'She has a beautiful face,' Maggie said suddenly, gazing at their patient. 'Yesterday it was beautiful,' she amended. 'Today she seems wasted, already burnt up.' There was a definite tremor in her voice, and Philip gave her a strange look. At the beginning of a long and exhausting operation he did not need his nurse getting emotional. It led to all kinds of problems, not least diminished concentration.

Maggie scrubbed at her arms, 'She looked as if she couldn't take the sort of operation you're describing.'

Every surgeon lived with the nightmare of having a patient die under his knife. Philip was no exception, but at this point he could not allow himself to think of it. His face was stony. 'Leave the theatre before you start cultivating your emotions,' he said harshly. His voice was gritty and tight; he was taking an awful risk and he knew it, Maggie knew it . . .

Polly Beardsley returned to her native New Zealand to begin her training as a nurse, after raising a family and many years travelling with a husband whose medical career took them to live in England, the USA, and the Far East. On graduating from Nursing School, Polly worked in a busy surgical ward as Staff Nurse and then in the operating theatre, before coming back to London to work in an inner city hospital. *On Call In Theatre* is her first Doctor–Nurse romance.

ON CALL IN THEATRE

BY

POLLY BEARDSLEY

MILLS & BOON LIMITED
ETON HOUSE 18–24 PARADISE ROAD
RICHMOND SURREY TW9 1SR

All the characters in this book have no existence outside the imagination of the Author, and have no relation whatsoever to anyone bearing the same name or names. They are not even distantly inspired by any individual known or unknown to the Author, and all the incidents are pure invention.

All rights reserved. The text of this publication or any part thereof may not be reproduced or transmitted in any form or by any means, electronic or mechanical, including photocopying, recording, storage in an information retrieval system, or otherwise, without the written permission of the publisher.

This book is sold subject to the condition that it shall not, by way of trade or otherwise, be lent, resold, hired out or otherwise circulated without the prior consent of the publisher in any form of binding or cover other than that in which it is published and without a similar condition including this condition being imposed on the subsequent purchaser.

*First published in Great Britain 1987
by Mills & Boon Limited*

© Polly Beardsley 1987

*Australian copyright 1987
Philippine copyright 1987*

ISBN 0 263 76013 8

Set in 10 on 10 pt Linotron Times
03–0288–61,100

*Photoset by Rowland Phototypesetting Limited
Bury St Edmunds, Suffolk
Made and printed in Great Britain by
William Collins Sons & Co Limited, Glasgow*

CHAPTER ONE

MARGARET BELL gave her fiancé an unhappy glance. 'I said I was sorry.'

'So am I, Maggie. I got the tickets you wanted for the show. I thought you were going to be off this evening. What happened?'

John Morton's voice was pleasant enough, but Maggie, sensing the hostility behind his words, suppressed a sigh. 'We had a case—I told you on the phone. It just took a lot longer than I expected . . . How was I to know you were going to wait for me?' she finished, looking at him helplessly. The silence was awful, as John sat poker-faced. 'Oh, John,' she protested, 'if you'd seen him! He's only four and he'd cut his fingers to the bone!' She paused, remembering the child's small distressed face with a shake of her curly head. 'Well, he came in before our duty was finished, so of course I scrubbed for the operation.'

'Good grief, Maggie, you're in charge of that theatre now! Why not get someone else to? You have other staff. Delegate.' He sighed, exasperated. 'Sometimes I think you can't know the meaning of the word!'

John's face, usually so restrained, was flushed and angry, and Maggie turned her head to stare through the car window at the bleak expanse of neon-lit streets. Beyond was the ancient brick tower of St Agnes' Hospital. It looked quiet, but in the windowless building in the back, the operating theatres were still working in a blaze of lights, she knew, for she had only just come off duty. Working late was an occupational hazard as far as she was concerned, but John, resenting the unpredictable hours, was unlikely ever to see it that way. If she were not so exhausted, she could handle him a lot better than she was doing, Maggie knew it.

'Look,' she said, in an effort to make him understand,

'I had this junior staff nurse on and I couldn't ask her to assist the consultant surgeon just so I could slip away, now could I? Anyway,' she reminded him, 'while Sister Campbell is on sick leave, I'm only acting charge.'

'Fair enough,' John admitted. But his concession was grudging. He was a big solid man who seldom showed his anger. Sometimes Maggie wished he would, instead of bottling it up. 'How is the little kid?' he asked.

'Oh, he came through the op fine,' said Maggie, glad he had asked. 'We don't know for certain whether he'll get back the use of his fingers, but we're hoping like crazy. With a surgeon like Philip Lonsdale, he has every chance.'

'Lonsdale would have to get good results to make up for that temper of his,' muttered John. But he took Maggie's slender hand in his. Slightly comforted, she leaned her head back against the car seat.

'It's tension, really,' she said at last. 'He gets wrapped up in his work, that's all. He's as hard on himself as he is with us, and he expects the sort of commitment he gives.' As she spoke, she was staring into space.

It was the most difficult job she had ever been asked to do. Since the day she had taken charge, every morning, from the moment she got up, she was fearful something would go terribly wrong, something she might have prevented if she were only more experienced. Too many cases crammed in, the long hours and tired staff; that kind of responsibility might have been easier to take, if the consultant had accepted her new role. He had not, although Maggie was as good as, if not better than any of the other nurses who had been in his theatre for as long.

For too many years, Fiona Campbell had sheltered Philip Lonsdale from the little crises that commonly occurred a dozen or so times a day, so that he was unaware of them. His concentration had been complete, he seldom had noticed the nurses—unless they did something wrong, that was, or very stupid, or got under his feet, in which case he noticed. He was totally unprepared for the day he suddenly found a pretty young thing with large silvery-grey eyes in charge of his theatre.

From the start, his barbed and subtle mind had cut the ground from beneath Maggie's feet. There was a way he had of making her feel too self-conscious, too tense and unsure of herself. Not that Maggie was unused to the quirkiness of the medical hierarchy. Although a shy girl, she nevertheless had a will of her own, and she could stand up for herself—a prime requisite, it seemed, for running an operating theatre.

Thank goodness John wasn't like Philip Lonsdale, she thought now. Her mood contrite, she whispered, 'I'm sorry I couldn't make it this evening, truly I am.'

John brightened immediately; he slid his arm around her shoulder drawing her close, his mouth seeking hers. She smiled, kissing him, but then as the pressure mounted, drew back. 'John,' she murmured, apology in her voice, 'I'd best be getting home, I'm on again first thing in the morning.'

'I knew it,' he muttered, his face taking on a sour look. He fidgeted irritably in his seat. 'How can we ever hope to have a life of our own when you insist on working these kind of hours?'

'It's not as if I do many afternoons and evenings,' Maggie protested. 'I'm usually eight in the morning till five at night, like anyone else.'

'Forgetting all the nights on call-back, aren't you?'

'Well, that goes with the job. And it's something you knew about when we got engaged.'

When they got engaged, she thought, with a sudden ache for how they had been then. Was it only four months ago? Can we have changed so much? she thought, miserable because she hated quarrelling. John thought she put her job first, and in a way it was understandable. But with this extra responsibility, she had to. Maggie could only hope that when Fiona returned, life would get back to normal. Their relationship, after all, wasn't any flash in the pan; it had grown out of a steady friendship and along with a comfortable certainty that they would settle down eventually, as man and wife. She had accepted John's proposal without surprise.

'Hey—you sleeping or sulking?'

'Idiot!' Maggie smiled and leaned over, resting against him lightly. 'The evening after next is yours,' she promised.

His mouth twisted. 'Don't tell me—no call-back?'

'Nope,' she said lightly, but registering the unpleasant look for the first time. She drew back and forced a laugh, 'Do I get to be driven home now, or not?'

'No choice in the matter, have I?' grumbled John, reaching nevertheless for the ignition key.

Maggie might have been troubled then, but John's sullen words did not prevent her from falling asleep the moment her head hit the pillow, and in the morning there was not a moment for any thoughts other than those concerning the day ahead.

Philip Lonsdale was the youngest consultant surgeon at St Agnes'. Tall, with fine aristocratic features and a head of loose black curls, he was considered by the nurses—those who did not have to work with him—to have the sexual magnetism of a Don Juan. The surgeon, however, was seemingly as uncaring about his good looks as he was about the effect he had on women. There was an aloofness about the man that set him apart.

They were waiting for him now, and Maggie's eyes were dark as she stood ready to tie Jane Richards' gown. Mentally she was checking through the preparations for the total knee replacement they were setting up for.

'Daydreaming again?' asked Jane, and Maggie chided, 'Get on—and stand still, for heaven's sake!'

'Hurry up then, he'll be here in a few minutes wanting to know why we're not ready. Thank God for Brad, is all I can say.'

Maggie did—and often. As an anaesthetist, Alan Bradford was the best. More importantly, as far as the nurses were concerned, he was approachable and friendly, and remained so through smooth and difficult days alike. His voice had become something of an institution, the deep somnolent tones inducing sleep in his patients and, less fortunately, the nurses who attended his lectures.

With Jane hitched and tied into place, Maggie opened the small sterile packs containing the doctors' gowns and pre-powdered gloves. She glanced up as Sue Manning, the newest member of the team, appeared hesitantly at the door. Maggie was well aware that the young staff nurse was finding the rigours and unpredictable tensions of an operating theatre hard to take, and she did not want to push her beyond her limits. She decided to put Sue with Jane that morning, as much to observe operation technique as to help. She herself would circulate —which meant, among other things, doing everything for the surgical team once they were scrubbed and enclosed within the surgical field.

Duncan Grant, Lonsdale's Registrar, pushed through the swing door. At his heels was Gary MacDonald, the young giant of a house surgeon known to the entire unit as 'Mac the Knife'—a nickname earned during an uninspired first week of surgery when he had inadvertently sliced the tip from Duncan's glove. Despite the teasing, Gary had survived to lean with a measure of confidence on the retractor and flirt with the nurses whenever he got the chance.

Duncan said morosely, 'Cas have got a motor-scooter prang-up. Girl—pretty mashed up, from all accounts. Lonsdale's round there now, assessing the damage.'

Gary cocked an eyebrow at Maggie before stationing himself at the sink next to Sue. Duncan's gloomy prognostications were well known. Alan Bradford thought he gave the theatre a bad name, and when Maggie watched the Registrar stooping over the operating table like some brooding bird of prey, she was inclined to agree with the anaesthetist.

'If she's as bad as they say we'll be getting her first. Better round up the arterial trays,' warned Duncan.

An extra orthopaedic pack, thought Maggie, bearing in mind the kind of injuries road accidents inflicted on limbs.

She was in the supplies room with her arms full when Philip Lonsdale passed by in the corridor. Seeing her, he stopped and came in, picking the heavy packs from her arms. His blue eyes were as cool and appraising as ever, and as watchful. The short-sleeved V-neck top he was wearing showed the muscular body of an athlete—a well-shaped head, determined jawline, strong neck and arms, still slightly tanned. His every movement oozed confidence—which Philip Lonsdale had in abundance.

'So this is where you're hiding!' The slight mocking humour in his voice implied that he never quite took Maggie seriously. The faintest of smiles curved his mouth—then it was gone. 'I've cancelled the knee, Sister,' he said crisply. 'We'll do this young woman first. She's pretty bad—lacerated arm, crushed leg; she'll need major arterial surgery as well as some knee reconstruction. I'll need you to scrub and assist me.'

Maggie took a steadying breath; the morning was shaping up to be really rough. 'Yes, sir. Er—Staff Nurse Richards is already scrubbed.'

'Good. We'll need her as well. Duncan will be doing the leg. Got somebody to circulate?'

'Er . . . yes.'

A touch of ice crept into the blue eyes. 'Well, have you or not? Never mind,' he said impatiently, dismissing the problem as Maggie's to sort out. 'Is the microscope set up?'

She had forgotten the microscope. 'No, sir,' she said, her mouth turning to gravel.

'Why not?'

'Because you don't use it routinely for knees,' Maggie pointed out, floundering under the steady gaze. 'It's usually left set up for the ENT theatre this afternoon,' she amended, somewhat inadequately, a dull flush beginning to colour her pale cheeks.

'Very convenient for Ear, Nose and Throat,' he observed caustically. 'However, I want it set up before the morning list. Every morning. That understood?'

'Yes, sir.' The microscope was the bane of Maggie's life. It towered in the corner of the big white-tiled theatre like some recalcitrant animal at bay. She was going to have to dismantle the E and T bits first . . .

'Where do you want this stuff?' he asked.

Maggie cleared a trolley and he placed the packs down. 'Don't forget the image intensifier as well.'

As well! Maggie fumed as he departed, then she grabbed some more drapes and fled along to the middle room to relay the change of plans to Sue and Jane.

'I've got to circulate!' said Sue, in a shocked whisper.

'Don't worry,' Maggie said hastily, 'we'll both help. Jane, I've got to go and do the microscope—can you manage everything here?'

'If we had an ODA you wouldn't need to,' Jane said unhelpfully.

'If pigs could fly,' Maggie muttered, helping peel a worried-looking staff nurse from her gown. Jane looked a shade too pale for Maggie's peace of mind, but there was no time now for anything other than encouraging noises. She did wonder, for the nth time, with considerable vexation, why Philip Lonsdale refused to allow them an operating department technician. Most of the other theatres were blessed with one.

As it was, it took a good twenty minutes for their patient to arrive. When she was wheeled into the anaesthetic room, Maggie went along, slipping into the room after the porters and casualty nurse had gone. Philip was already there, talking to her quietly. Alan Bradford and his nurse, Bronwyn Evans, were searching with unhurried intensity for a suitable vein to carry a wide-bore blood needle.

Maggie let her mask slip around her neck and went to stand beside Philip Lonsdale. He raised his eyes under the heavy brows. 'Here's Sister Bell,' he said, his tone gentle now, reserved for the patient. The girl on the trolley looked pitifully young, her eyes open and glassy —there was a haunting quality in them that Maggie would remember for the rest of her life. She struggled to keep her face calmly smiling, when it wanted to twist into a spasm of compassion for the hideous mass of scraped skin and bone down one side of the girl's face.

'All right, love,' she said, her voice not quite steady. 'We'll soon have you off to sleep.'

Alan had found his vein. 'You'll feel a little prick . . .

there's a good girl!' He slid in the needle, Bronwyn sealed it down with tape and snapped off the tourniquet. The hypodermic syringe was ready. 'Count up to ten for me, love.'

Maggie watched the lashes flutter, the trim little jaw slacken; she stayed by Philip's side as Alan swiftly took his patient through the stages of anaesthesia induction. When he was satisfied she was fully comatosed, he nodded, and Philip drew back the covers.

Nothing ever quite prepared Maggie for the jolt terrible injuries brought. She turned her face momentarily from the blood-soaked pads. Philip's face was grim, and burdened with care. 'It'll be touch and go with that arm,' he said to Alan.

Maggie reached for the notes. 'Beth Liddell, aged twenty-two,' she read. Twenty-two, she thought, her own age. Her eyes dropped to the crushed leg where the girl's clothes were sodden with dangerously escaping body fluids.

'Let's get these jeans off—we'll have to cut them.'

Maggie responded with a start to Philip's voice; she tore the drawer open and produced the scissors. When they had finished, Philip made a swift examination. 'Just as I thought,' he said, straightening. 'The knee-cap's a total write off. I'll go and get scrubbed.' For a moment he continued to look down at the injured leg, then abruptly he strode away.

Barely a moment later the theatre doors swung open and Sue Manning hurried through. She stopped, her eyes wide. Half turning away, she muttered, 'Oh, my God!'

Maggie thought she was going to faint; it wouldn't be the first time a theatre nurse had come crashing to the floor. Quickly she moved, her hand outstretched. 'It's all right,' Sue said shakily, though her eyes were strangely fixed.

'Sit her down,' said Alan from behind, and Bronwyn shoved a chair under her. Sue's legs gave way and she sat down with a plump. 'He—he wants some kind of instrument, I—I don't know . . .'

Bronwyn and Maggie exchanged looks; an hysterical nurse was all they needed. 'Sue, stop it! It's all right,' Maggie said calmly, and feeling far from that happy state. 'I'll see to Mr Lonsdale. If you like, I can ask for someone to take over from you—what do you say?'

'No—please, I'm fine now,' Sue said quickly.

Maggie gave her arm a comforting squeeze, her fears somewhat allayed by the girl's determined look. 'OK—well, if you're sure. I'll go and see what he wants, I've got to go and get scrubbed anyway. Dr Bradford and Bronwyn will tell you anything you want to know, positioning, things like that.'

Philip Lonsdale waited impatiently in the scrub room with gloved hands clasped at chest level, his eyes flashing electric blue over his mask as Maggie entered. 'What's the matter with that nurse? I ask her something and she disappears,' he growled.

Maggie prudently refrained from any explanation and darted round behind him to tie the tapes at his back. She had to stand on tiptoe to reach the top, where the gown edges did not quite close across the broad shoulders. With the last tie knotted, he shrugged, as much as to say she had taken too long about it. 'See that I have the screw-lock diathermy forceps on hand,' was all he said as he strode into the theatre to join the others already waiting.

Six minutes later Maggie was gowned, masked and gloved, and relieved to find there was still a little time with which to check her instrument tables and take a count with Sue. She was a diminutive figure, brilliantly lighted by the big overhead lamp, her fine fly-away red hair completely covered by the tight theatre cap which emphasised the stem-frailty of her neck, as much as the long green gown reaching almost to her toes.

Many times during the past months Maggie had scrubbed as instrument nurse for Philip Lonsdale. She knew the way he worked and was able to anticipate his needs, so that he never had to glance up. She would have the instrument ready, everything in quick succession the way he wanted. There was a sensitive, intuitive rhythm between them, a confidence in the way Maggie placed a scalpel or forceps or dissector in his hands, releasing the instant his grip was secure on it.

Until Fiona Campbell went off sick, Philip had not been aware of Maggie other than as a pair of gloved hands. Her efficiency had shielded her. And then one day in the middle of an operation, he had paused, to look at her very deliberately. Maggie had felt the heat creep right up her throat and spread in a hectic stain beneath her mask. Stripped of her anonymity, her awareness of him heightened, and along with it an uncomfortable feeling that she could do nothing right. Often now she would find his dark, deep, deep blue eyes on her in a brooding stare.

'Ready,' she heard Alan say, and she glanced up. Beth Liddell was only semi-recognisable now, with the endotracheal tubing and mask distorting her features. Philip nodded for them to get on with it and as Jane stepped up to the table opposite, Maggie handed over one end of a sterile drape. They worked silently and rapidly until the operating sites were enclosed within rectangles of green. Maggie moved her instrument tables in and Sue, responding to silent directions, drew in the kick buckets in their wheeled frames, then tackled the microscope. Getting it exactly right took precious minutes. At last it was positioned where Philip could control the eyepiece himself when he wanted. His nod was brief, and Sue's flushed, worried face disappeared from the operative field. Maggie took her position, leaving Jane to cope with Duncan and Gary, and the long tedious operation to join nerves and blood vessels and torn tissues began.

They settled down to the routine, Philip probing gently with his forceps for foreign bodies. As blood began to flood from an artery, he clamped it, saying tersely, 'Suction.'

Maggie was ready with the nozzle. She cleared the area of blood, then prepared a suture needle. Philip looked up at the anaesthetist.

'Lab came through with the packed cells?'

'Not yet,' said Alan, as imperturbable as ever. 'We're running through a unit of whole blood.'

'Up to you,' Philip pointed out, with weighted precision, 'but I'd get them on the ball. We're going to need those units, and more.' He gestured for the needle and went back to repairing the artery, his gloved hands moving with infinite patience and delicacy, seemingly oblivious at having disturbed the anaesthetic department—whose job blood was—out of its normal complacency.

'Clamp that little blighter over there. Got it?'

'I think so,' Maggie said gravely.

A glint of a smile in the blue eyes. 'Good girl!'

The packed cells went up and they worked on in the race against time. Every so often Philip would glance up at the transfusion line, then at the growing pile of empty blood bags. At last he stepped back and rinsed his gloved hands. 'Think we're winning, Brad?'

'That blood pressure's too low,' Alan said, with a slow shake of his head. He cast an expert eye over the lines of dripping swabs hanging from the racks, assessing the loss. 'Losing more than we can pump in.'

Philip turned to look at his Registrar. Duncan's pinched, pale face reflected the colour of his gown under the artificial lighting; beads of perspiration stood on his brow, only to reappear the moment Sue mopped them up. 'We've re-established blood supply, but it's shaky.'

A muscle pulsating under Philip Lonsdale's left eye was the only indication he gave of the tension underlying his calm. He made his decision. 'Right, let's get her off the table. We'll have to bring her back later . . . if she can stand it,' he added ominously. 'Finish tying off and close up.' He turned back, hand outstretched. Maggie placed the needle-holder in it and nodded for Sue Manning to take the final count.

Looking flustered, Sue joined her at the instrument table. They started with the used needles. Finishing, Sue glanced at her clipboard, then up at the wall where she had marked down the needles given out during the operation. 'Should be fifteen—I'm one short,' she said unhappily.

Maggie looked up, counting the marks. 'You didn't mark the second to last,' she said. Philip glanced up with a darted look.

'I'm closing up, so don't tell me the count's wrong.'

Damn, Maggie thought, he must have ears like a bat. 'Hurry, Sue,' she whispered. They started on the swabs, then the sharps and small instruments, all of which tallied. Sue, glad to get it over with, backed away, nearly upsetting a washbasin in her haste.

'All correct, sir,' Maggie said quickly, and met the answering narrowed look with relief.

Beth Liddell was still asleep, but the muscle relaxant being supplied intravenously was wearing off, and she started to move, her muscles convulsing. Alan whipped out the endotracheal tube, cleared her mouth and throat by suction and inserted an airway. He replaced the mask, giving pure oxygen, and gave the black reservoir bag on the machine a few quick pumps to assist her breathing. They stood waiting, watching, as the bag hung limp, and Maggie felt her stomach begin to knot up. Then, as Beth's chest started to rise and fall, the bag slowly inflated.

'She's breathing on her own, let's get her on the bed,' said Alan.

The porter came forward with the waiting bed. They all helped lift, Philip doing his share before going to write up his notes, Alan managing the head and short Bronwyn wrestling to get the intravenous bottles up on the bed stand. Gary, towering over her, took them with a grin and hooked them easily in place. When Philip was satisfied that they had Beth positioned correctly, Alan replaced the heavy black mask with a green transparent Hudson and linked it to the portable oxygen machine that would travel with them. Most patients went on one of the theatre trolleys to Recovery, but Beth's condition was critical and she was being transferred straight to the intensive care unit.

Maggie stripped her gloves and pulled paper shoes

over her clogs. As she gathered the charts and snatched down the X-rays from their lighted box, Philip shoved the operation notes into her hand.

'Tell Sister I'll be along in a few minutes.' Maggie nodded, then ran to catch up with the procession making its way along the corridor.

Jane was clearing up by the time she got back. 'We're to have morning tea,' she informed Maggie. 'I've sent Sue and Bronny to have theirs. Lord, I didn't think Sue was going to make it there for a while, did you?'

Maggie threw her gown in the bin and went to help straighten the theatre for the next case. 'She did very well,' she called back.

In the common room Bronwyn and Gary were enjoying the first real laugh of the morning. Gary was in his favourite position on the old sway-backed couch, feet up on the end. He said, as Maggie and Jane appeared, 'Maggie'll know.'

'Know what?' asked Maggie, heading with unseemly haste for the steaming urn and savouring the delectable aroma of freshly made coffee.

'Mother Fee's taking long leave. True or false?' Gary asked.

Fiona Campbell had only just left the hospital after eight days' post-hysterectomy and could reasonably be expected to convalesce for another six weeks before being expected to return. Maggie said as much. But Bronwyn shook her small dark head. 'Oh no. We heard it was more like a year she's going to be away.'

'A year?' Jane queried. 'First we've heard of it. When did we last see her, Maggie? Two days? Fee never mentioned it.'

Maggie poured two cups and handed one to Jane. 'Help, I hope it's not a year! Six weeks of this is about as much as I'll be able to stand!'

Duncan eased his long frame cautiously on to one of their new, spiky-looking chairs, and commented, 'I wouldn't think you had any worries. Theatre's running well.'

Seemingly Theatre ran itself. No one ever mentioned

the balancing act it required to keep it running at all, let alone running smoothly. Maggie was silent. People only notice if things go wrong, she was thinking—in which case it was her fault, and the whole world knew about it.

Jane gave her a wink. 'There's nursing for you—you never get any of the credit!'

Gary dug into the pocket of his crumpled greens and produced a packet of cigarettes, ignoring as usual the No Smoking sign on the wall.

'Maggie gets my vote—but when you see old Fee again, tell her I was asking after her health.' He always liked to hedge his bets.

Duncan, who didn't smoke, gave an infuriated chortle. 'Most likely you're the reason for poor Fee's hormonal imbalance,' he said, in a nasty reference to Gary's devil-may-care attitude. As far as Duncan was concerned, Gary did not fit his idea of how conscientious a surgeon, even one in the making, should be. He often wondered why Philip tolerated him.

'Cut it out!' protested Gary. 'Fibroids, wasn't it, Maggie? For Pete's sake, not every woman has a hysterectomy because of hormonal imbalance.'

Philip Lonsdale's appearance effectively put an end to the argument, for Duncan, drinking the rest of his tea in one gulp, stood up with the clear intention of getting back to work—an action which prompted Gary to at least pocket his unlit cigarette. Bronwyn pulled her mouth down in a sympathetic look that linked the two against the uncaring world of the non-smoker, and melted back to the anaesthetic department where their next patient would be waiting.

Alan would be there himself, after taking tea with the unit staff, and Maggie reluctantly nodded for Sue to go and start her scrub, and as the girl went, consternation darkening her expression, she wondered how long she would last with them. She needs taking under a wing, someone like Fiona, she thought. Maggie hoped the rumour was untrue.

'I'll go with her,' muttered Jane, and followed Sue out. Gary departed also and Maggie found herself alone with Philip. Rather hastily she put down her cup, preparing to retreat. Conversation, she had found, was not easy with the consultant.

'Don't rush away, Sister Bell.'

Maggie paused, her stomach giving its customary twinge as the blue eyes probed her.

'You were lucky with that needle count. One missing, and it might have been a different story. There's no time to muck about looking for lost equipment when a patient's life is hanging in the balance.'

She knew that—he needn't rub it in. She shifted on to her other foot; she considered cracking the old joke about clamps and gold cigarette cases being left inside a patient—and thought better of it. Fiona Campbell might have got away with it, but Maggie doubted very much if she would.

'It wasn't exactly lost,' she ventured. 'I knew how many needles we'd used.'

'You may have, but the circulating nurse didn't have a clue. Isn't it her job to keep track of what she hands out?'

Immediately Maggie was on the defensive. 'Well, yes, but Staff's only learning, and she was rushed off her feet.'

'If a nurse can't cope under stress, then she shouldn't be working in an operating theatre,' Philip said repressively.

'If it was anybody's fault, it was mine,' Maggie said rashly. 'I shouldn't have pushed her into circulating so soon.'

'Then why did you?'

The question was directed like a missile. The fact was, in a situation as fraught as they had that morning, it was dangerous to have anyone on the team who was not utterly sure of what they were doing, and why. And Philip Lonsdale knew that better than anybody, as he waited for Maggie to answer. Her clear grey eyes had shifted anxiously to his face. She was too damn young to have such responsibility thrust upon her, Philip thought, in a sudden inexplicable rage. Damned hospital administrators—they didn't care who they ruined in the process of keeping their low-level staffing policy.

'There was no one else,' Maggie admitted at last. 'We don't often have the situation where two nurses are scrubbed at the same time.'

He knew it. They were low on staff. 'You had only to ask Paula, she would have found you an experienced nurse,' he said. He knew Paula Crisp, she could always find one—where from, he had no idea.

Maggie's face was strained. It was all very well for him to say! She had seen the sick list that day, and the Theatre Supervisor couldn't pull extra staff out of a hat. Besides, she thought, Sue had done really well in the circumstances.

Philip saw her proud little head come up with a sudden return of assurance. 'It wasn't necessary to get anyone else,' she said. 'Nurse Manning has my fullest confidence and I was happy with the job she did.'

She stood her ground, her cheeks hot—it was not quite true; she had been, and still was, terribly worried about Sue. But the fact remained that Sue had done a good job, surprisingly good, in a situation far more complex than usual. She had to have her chance.

Philip knew she was hiding the truth in a mistaken loyalty. If the girl was unsuitable, let her go. He sighed. He wasn't in charge of the theatre, that was the Nursing department—though his opinions counted, of course.

At last, disconcerted by the protracted silence, Maggie cleared her throat nervously. 'Do you think Beth Liddell will pull through?' she ventured.

'Probably,' Philip said shortly, his face unreadable. 'I wouldn't like to bet on that leg, though.'

'You mean it might have to be amputated?' Maggie queried, appalled.

He sighed. 'Let's hope not, shall we?'

Maggie nodded silently, and because he seemed to have forgotten her presence, turned to go.

'Won't you stay and have a cup with me?' Philip asked, and saw the look of surprise in her eyes as she turned back. He was smiling, and Maggie thought, curiously wistful, if only he did that more often. But she declined with a little shake of her head. 'Thanks, I must be getting back.'

'You did a good job this morning.'

'Oh . . . thank you.' She flushed with pleasure.

She left him thoughtfully stirring his coffee and hurried along to the theatre. The day's surgical list was still ahead of them, and there were a dozen things that needed her immediate attention.

CHAPTER TWO

MAGGIE pulled off her cap and massaged her eyes briefly. She was tired, dog-tired. In fact, she felt numb with tiredness, rather as if she herself had been anaesthetised. Yawning until her eyes watered, she asked Jane, who was spreadeagled in the one chair the changing room possessed, 'You don't think Brad can have got careless with the halothane and given us all a dose, do you?' Sometimes she wondered about the calm, almost euphoric atmosphere prevailing in the anaesthetic department.

'Are you kidding? We're tired because Philip Lonsdale is working us into the ground. You count up the number of cases we put through today, and not counting Beth Liddell.' Jane stripped off her cap. 'Do you know, that man's on call practically every night this week. Other consultants make their Registrars do that sort of thing, why can't he? I know old Duncan has a mass of kids at home—all the same . . .' She looked at Maggie. 'Think he's trying to cut down on the waiting list single-handed?'

Maggie remained staring thoughtfully into space. Jane was wondering if she had gone off to sleep, when Maggie shrugged and pulled some clothes from her locker rung. 'Don't ask me. According to Fiona Campbell, work is all he cares about.'

'Great. But do we all have to suffer?' grumbled Jane. She twitched at her hair, peering into the long mirror opposite. 'What am I going to do with it? Tell me,' she said, holding out a mousy strand for inspection.

Jane's hair was wispy, there was no other word for it. Worse, the head-hugging caps they were obliged to wear on duty mercilessly flattened what little she had. It did not help that Maggie's wild tangle of curls survived to bounce up in full glory at the end of the day.

Maggie gave her a considered look. 'I'd have it cut very short—say about an inch all over—to show off the shape of your head.'

'Thanks,' muttered Jane. 'Then I'd look like Roland Rat.'

Maggie gave up. She knew Jane's mood of old. They finished dressing in silence until Jane said, with an impish grin, 'Last one out's a cabbage!' and they both made a mad rush for the door.

Home was rented accommodation in a terraced house a mere five minutes from the hospital. Maggie and Jane each had their own bedroom, the rest of the house they shared with the owner, Nigel Spence. It had been a lucky find, because rooms in that part of London came expensive, and usually for more than a nurse's salary allowed.

The living-room was generously proportioned, the kitchen large enough to accommodate a table for six, and best of all, there was a little garden outside the back door where there was a bird table and space for a couple of chairs.

Reaching the house, Jane paused with the key in the door. 'I hope Nigel is out and we get the place to ourselves for a change,' she said.

Maggie agreed. Nigel was all right, but when he was at home it seemed to be open house for all his trendy friends—something his considerable income as interior designer made possible. Nigel was happiest when the house was buzzing with scintillating chatter, everybody talking at once and no one listening; whereas Maggie and Jane longed for some peace and quiet after the controlled hysteria of a normal day in the operating theatre.

About to put a foot on the stairs, she heard Nigel's voice calling from the back. The girls exchanged looks. 'Come on—I feel like tea anyway,' said Jane.

Nigel was in the kitchen wearing his shiny white vinyl apron, imprinted with black lace bra and suspender belt in appropriate places. He took up the cocktail mixer when he saw them. 'Glasses in the ice-box, kiddies.'

Nigel always referred to the fridge as the ice-box, and like the apron, they scarcely noticed any more. 'Not in my condition, Nigel—believe me, one of your Martinis would flatten me. I'll die, though, if I don't get a cuppa,' Jane said, and Maggie headed for the kettle,

'Me too, thanks anyway,' she said.

Nigel tilted his narrow jaw and pouted. 'Sure? One of my cocktails would do more for you girls.' His hair was looking very well groomed, and several shades blonder, Maggie was sure. It gave him a slightly washed-out appearance, and she longed to tell him to leave it dark, it would suit him so much better.

'Expecting anyone?' asked Jane, on the threshold at the fridge, her eyes on the plates of food inside.

Nigel's smile was embarrassed. 'There's a little party tonight,' he said, rather belatedly. 'So don't forget to dress.'

Jane laughed. 'Like in pyjamas. Sorry, Nige, I'm for bed early tonight, round about sevenish, going by the way I feel!'

Maggie declined as well. She wondered what Nigel would do if they did turn up. He was always asking them, but it was only form. The phone rang and she went into the hall to pick it up, knowing the call would probably be for Nigel, and was surprised to hear John's voice on the line. John made a point of phoning only once, and that was during the evening, and then only if they had not already met that day. He tended to regard phoning as unnecessary, as well as an added expense, at a time when they were both saving up to put a deposit on a flat.

'John, is that you?' she asked.

'Who did you expect?' he teased.

He sounded in a good mood, Maggie thought, surprised at how relieved that made her. 'Well, nobody,' she laughed. 'I mean, you don't usually call at this time . . .'

'Then I'm not such a creature of habit as you thought. Listen, Maggie, my parents will be here tomorrow and I want you to meet them. I thought we could get together at, say, six-thirty, if that's not too early for you, then go on somewhere for dinner at eight.'

'They're not expected for ages yet, surely?' Maggie queried.

'Maggie, we're getting married soon. I'd like them to meet you before the actual day.'

'Yes, of course. It just goes to show how time flies!' Maggie gave a small hysterical laugh, her mind already on what she should wear. Her cream linen suit would be the most suitable; she wondered if there was time to get it to the cleaners. And her hair? She raked nervous fingers through it. She knew how John liked her hair to be short and neat. Presumably his parents would as well, and she did want to give a good impression.

'You are off duty tomorrow evening?' John asked suddenly.

'Oh yes, no problem. I was thinking what a mess my hair is, that's all.'

'It'll be fine, now don't worry. Can you make it for six-thirty?'

Maggie agreed she could and after a few more words, hung up. Jane came past carrying a tray laden with tea things. She nodded her head towards the stairs and Maggie followed willingly, her mouth watering at the sight of a plate piled high with dripping toast.

They chose Jane's room. It was slightly bigger than Maggie's, and even then one had to sit on the bed as there was space only for a lone chintz chair.

'Gosh!' Jane exclaimed, when Maggie told her. 'His parents!'

'Uh-huh. Do you think the cream linen will do? It's still so wintry.'

'Wear my camel over it,' Jane offered. She produced a jar of strawberry preserves. 'Here, help yourself.'

Maggie took a liberal spoonful. 'What can I do with my hair?' she fretted. 'It needs a good trim, do you think?'

Jane gave her a long look. 'Nothing wrong with your hair. Stop using it as an excuse.'

'I'm doing nothing of the sort,' said Maggie, a trifle

tetchily. 'Well,' she admitted after a lengthy pause, 'I suppose I am in a way.' She looked at Jane, her grey eyes troubled, then a sparkle appeared. 'Just you wait, one day your prospective in-laws will turn up, and then we'll see the flap you get in!'

Jane pulled a face. 'I'm waiting.' She was very self-conscious about her appearance—mousy, rather stocky. She sighed. 'Go on, have some more toast, and stop worrying. One look at you and they'll thank their lucky stars their son has had the good sense to choose you.'

Maggie wondered, but she said nothing. If she had doubts, she had not mentioned them, and it was getting a bit late in the day to do so now. She shoved her thoughts aside. Then, as usually happened, they started talking shop. Several cups of tea later, and feeling more rested, Maggie made her way to her own room.

It was only just six o'clock, and already the night had closed in. She crossed the room to switch on the lamp above her high narrow bed, then stood by the window a moment, contemplating the February streets. A perceptible chill came off the dank glass and she pulled the plum-coloured velveteen curtains with a shiver. Pensive, she went to her wardrobe and brought out the linen suit, then holding it tight against her, she surveyed the effect in the mirror.

It was an expensive suit, a present from her father, on one of his rare visits to London. At first Maggie was dubious about the wide padded shoulders. He had urged her to try it on and she had, and found to her delight that she was tall enough to get away with them. In fact, the severely tailored style proved a perfect foil for her intense femininity, and the pale shade of cream was just right. Too right, Maggie thought, yearning to wear wild pinks and outrageous plums.

But, when one had hair like hers, the colour of a copper jam pan, not red and not gold, a colour which defied description and inclined to frizz into the bargain, well then, it was best to stick to quiet colours. Against the mass of rich hair her face was pale and wraith-like, her mouth soft and vulnerable, the corners were apt to turn down, as they did now.

What did it matter? she thought, shrugging. John's parents were coming to see her, not inspect her wardrobe. But she remained staring at the mirror, her eyes far away. She was thinking about Philip Lonsdale. When he had looked at her, smiling like that, his eyes a deep, intense blue, she had known the strangest feeling.

She stirred, frowning, and hung up the suit. All the same, a nagging restlessness possessed her, and after half an hour of indecision she decided to go and visit Fiona.

Jane was washing her hair. She lifted her head dripping from the basin in surprise. 'I thought you were too tired for anything other than bed?' she commented.

'Well, I did sort of promise,' Maggie said vaguely. 'Want to come?'

Jane groped for a towel. 'Look, if you don't mind, I won't. Tell you what, though, I'll have a bite of supper ready for when you get back.'

Fiona Campbell lived in a pleasant little flat overlooking the Thames, and Maggie found her padding about the kitchen in mules and a housecoat. She was a thin woman of about forty-two, with a sallow complexion and tired eyes. They brightened when she saw Maggie bearing a bright posy of early narcissi. While Fiona arranged the flowers, Maggie sat at the kitchen table telling her all the hospital news. Later, they went to sit by the gas fire in the sitting-room. 'I've decided to go and see my daughter in Australia,' Fiona announced, as they settled with a glass of wine. 'It's about time, I haven't seen her since she got married.'

'So it is true—you are taking long leave!' Maggie exclaimed.

'That's the hospital grapevine for you! It knows your business before you do,' Fiona observed tartly. 'But yes, it is true.'

'Just something Gary Mac said this morning,' Maggie explained, wishing she hadn't said anything at all. 'He sends his regards,' she added.

'He would! The rascal spends far too much time trying

to bed the young nurses and not enough on his work.' Fiona scowled, then winked. 'Take no notice, Maggie—I'm turning into one of those old bats! Between us, though, that blessed op took it out of me.'

'It would anybody,' Maggie hastened to assure her. 'Your trouble is, you don't expect to react like a normal patient.'

'Perhaps.' Fiona raked her hair back in a tired gesture, and Maggie was shocked to see how grey the roots were.

'Your daughter will be pleased you're going,' she said.

'I hope so!' Fiona laughed, then laid her square capable hand on the arm rest and leaned over, her attention on Maggie. 'Paula tells me you're making a go of it.'

That was a compliment, coming from Paula, Maggie supposed. Her lips twitched into a wide smile.

'If I take long leave, they'll have to appoint somebody in my place permanently, you know that.' Fiona paused for emphasis. 'Why not apply yourself?'

Maggie stared at her. 'Fee, I don't think I could cope.'

'Nonsense—you are, apparently,' Fiona interrupted.

'Oh, yes, at the moment. But that's because you had everybody so well trained. As they go and new ones come on, I think I might be in trouble. I'm not—well, not . . .'

'A tyrant,' Fiona finished for her.

'Yes—I mean no,' said Maggie, going red. It was true, though, Fee did run the theatre like a military exercise. She just did it so well no one noticed. 'Well, anyway, I couldn't, not with getting married and all. It might have been different if John understood how it was, I don't know, and I have the feeling he wants me to give up full-time work.'

'That's a pity,' muttered Fiona. 'But for heaven's sake, don't go and ruin your marriage for the sake of a career. I did. And it's not worth it, not in the long run. I think a lot of women are finding that out.' She uttered a small, ragged laugh. 'There's a high price to pay for freedom, Maggie.'

Dear Fee! The one they took their problems to—

always competent and in control, always available. But at what expense? Maggie wondered, ashamed the way they had taken it all for granted.

Sensing Maggie's sympathy, Fiona adopted a fierce no-nonsense kind of look and continued in a more conversational tone, 'Of course, it goes the other way too. Look at Philip Lonsdale. His wife couldn't stand the fact that he spent all his time with NHS patients—though I think it would have been hunky-dory if the money was rolling in from Private—anyway, she up and left him to join the jet set. Mind you, she always liked the good times. I knew her in the old days, would you believe. Come to think of it, I knew Philip when he was a long-haired medical student. Well, that's another story. I must say, though, I feel sorry for the son.'

Maggie, whose stomach had lurched in a quite curious manner at the mention of his name, said, 'I didn't know Philip had a son.'

'Well, he has. Nice little kid—he's at boarding school, I believe. Philip has custody and that makes madam furious, of course, but if the truth be known, she doesn't want to be bothered with a child.' Fiona sighed. 'What a mess we make of our lives! We don't know what we want half the time, and when we do, it's too late.' She looked across at Maggie. 'And that's the thing, you have to be sure of what it is you do want.'

Maggie brooded all the way home on the bus. She wasn't sure—that was the trouble. Before going to bed that night, she pulled out the photograph taken on her father's wedding day and looked at it carefully. Her mother had been sure, it shone from her face. And her father—lean, strong, lively eyes, a mouth full of humour, his bride's hand clasped in his; there was no uncertainty there, just pride and love. Her mother had died when Maggie was five, and her father had never married again. How he must have loved her, Maggie thought, looking at him. She put the photograph back.

As usual, she saw they got to the hospital in plenty of time the next morning. Being early gave a feeling of being one jump ahead, and she needed all the advantage she could get. The surgical list was up on the board in the duty room, and Jane ran a practised eye down the operations scheduled for the day. 'All minor cases,' she said at last. 'Duncan will be doing this lot,' adding hopefully, 'Think we could scrounge a cup of coffee before he arrives?'

'Fat chance,' said Bronwyn, arriving in a rush. Maggie automatically handed over the drug cupboard keys. 'What's the big hurry?' she enquired.

'Lonsdale is here. He's doing the list, for God's sake. Duncan is over at Mary's lecturing. Poor Brad, he had to leave half his breakfast.'

Jane looked at Maggie. 'Well, what are we standing here for?'

Philip was methodically drying his arms with a sterile towel Maggie presumed he must have had to get, and open, himself. She was treated to a withering glance that was in no way leavened by the usual good-morning smile. He turned back to his task. 'I thought we might have got an early start today, Sister.' As though the cause was hopelessly beyond saving now.

Feeling already damned, Maggie directed a furious glance at the broad uncompromising back before moving directly through to the middle room, leaving Jane to cope with his needs.

The room was a shambles and she groaned aloud; it was going to take time to sort out. There had been a string of acute cases the previous evening and the girls on the one-to-nine shift had not much time to spare on preparations for the morning list. Consequently trolleys were crammed in any old how, and most of them overflowed with autoclaved packs so that Maggie had first to sort out where to begin before she could start opening up for their number one case. She gritted her teeth; there was nothing for it but to plunge in—from then on she lost all track of time in the endless rush. They had a struggle to keep up, for unlike Duncan who plodded, Philip was as fast as he was thorough. It was, as Alan Bradford cheerfully remarked, a day when they went like the clappers.

There was a brief respite for morning coffee, and half an hour in which to bolt lunch. Jane complained on the way back that her stomach felt like so much concrete —'It might be, for all we know,' she added, in a dark reference to the cafeteria food.

But Maggie's thoughts were on Sue Manning, who was flagging badly. They had done their best to guide her through the hectic morning, but if anything, Sue seemed less confident than ever. 'What can we do?' Maggie asked.

'Get her to scrub for the afternoon cases.'

'I would,' Maggie said uncertainly. 'If it were Duncan . . .'

'Maggie, it's the only way to learn, you know it is. You're too soft. If Sue doesn't shape up or ship out, the Theatre Super will.'

That convinced Maggie—no fate could be worse than that. But Sue wasn't as easy to convince, 'I can't seem to hand things the right way,' she said unhappily.

'It'll come,' Maggie assured her. 'Be firm, don't slap them in like you see on films. Don't tickle his palm either. After a few times you'll wonder what you were worried about.'

Sue fidgeted with her stack of drapes, giving the table nervous glances, as if it might up and bite her. 'I'll never remember what I'm supposed to do next,' she sighed.

'Yes, you will. Take it quietly, essentials first. Knife, fork and spoon, always remember that.'

'What?' exclaimed Sue, more bewildered than ever.

'Skin knife, scissors, artery forceps,' Maggie explained patiently. 'Put those out first. And you know about keeping your dirty things separate—skin knife straight into the dirty kidney dish and it isn't used again—always have a couple of artery forceps where he can grab them. Jane will be standing right by you—and don't worry, he'll ask for anything he wants.'

'He'll be hoarse before too long,' said Sue, still fretful but looking rather more composed, Maggie was relieved to note.

'We've got throat lozenges,' said Jane, and looked

across at Maggie. 'What have you done with the X-rays? He wants them.'

'Forgotten to put them up, haven't I? You stay with Sue, I'll see to it.'

Maggie found Philip Lonsdale standing in the theatre waiting for the next case to arrive, gloved hands tightly clasped, his face registering a pained look. With Sue assisting, it was unlikely to disappear either, Maggie thought. She laid down a large brown envelope and drew out several X-rays, slotting them carefully into the wall fixture, and turned the light on. Philip gave them a cursory glance. 'Now, if you can possibly find the recent ones. These were taken of an old injury . . . unless you think I ought to perform the same operation twice?'

'Oh, sorry—yes, here are the latest.' Maggie quickly replaced the out-of-date films and stood back.

'Better,' he conceded. 'If we could have them the right way up . . .' Maggie was already doing just that, 'Ah yes, that's more helpful.' Sarcastic so-and-so! she thought, breathing hard. She stood ready to insert any other, as required, while Philip continued to study the films in front of him.

'That's fine. Now can I have Beth Liddell's X-rays?'

'I'll have the unit send them along,' said Maggie, preparing to go; there were a dozen and one things she still had to do before the start of their next case. His next words came like a bolt from the blue.

'If you would. I'm bringing her back. These minor cases won't take long. I'd like you to set up for arterial surgery as soon as we finish so we can get started by five.'

He couldn't! She was meeting John and his parents at six-thirty. In a panic she saw them waiting, and waiting, and . . . then she remembered the one-to-nine team. Of course, it was their job anyway to take acute cases after their afternoon list was finished. She pointed this out with a measure of confidence, convinced she had found the solution.

'Thank you for reminding me, Sister.'

Maggie's eyes lifted fearfully to his face. He glowered at her. 'They won't be finished before seven, at the earliest, that's why I'm asking you to get started—however painfully aware I am of your hours, I need you as my instrument nurse. The others can swop without much difficulty.' Now! Now—tell him now, Maggie told herself. But she remained rooted to the spot, her mouth slightly open, and uttered not a word. 'Naturally,' he added, 'you'll be able to claim overtime.'

Overtime? Maggie flushed; she had never claimed overtime in her life. A small rebellious streak caused her head to come up even further.

'It's not possible. I'm going out this evening,' she said, and as he raised a puzzled brow, as if wondering what that had to do with him, she added desperately, 'It's all arranged.'

'I'm sorry,' he said stiffly, noting the stubborn set to her mouth—a passionate mouth, he observed—and taking into account also the red hair escaping in tiny curls on her hairline. That colouring, always the sign of an excitable temperament. She was quite unsuited to her present position of authority, the tyranny of which would wear her down in the end. But she was the best scrub nurse they had. He sighed, wishing he did have the choice. 'I'm sorry,' he said again, more gently, 'but unfortunately Beth's condition will not permit us the luxury of waiting those extra two hours. If I did, her foot would turn gangrenous.'

'Oh.' Maggie felt she had let him down. Ashamed, she said, 'Then of course there's no question.' She finalised some details with him and hurried away, only realising then that she had forgotten to tell him about Sue and putting in a good word for her.

'He wouldn't be subjecting Beth to surgery so soon unless it was absolutely necessary,' she told Jane. 'But what am I to do?'

'About what?'

'Meeting John and his parents, what did you think?' Maggie almost snapped, thinking that sometimes Jane went out of her way to be infuriating. 'If her circulation is impaired, it will mean a graft, and that could take hours—not counting work on her knee.'

'Phone him and explain,' Jane said shortly, her eyes deliberately lowered, and Maggie wondered suddenly if she wasn't the teeniest bit jealous that she was never asked to assist. But she dismissed the thought immediately. She would have known about it, Jane never managed to keep a secret for long. 'Slip out now,' said Jane, recovering her usual sunny expression, 'I'll stand in for you.'

'He'll be furious,' Maggie said uneasily, dithering.

'Well, that's his problem, but you'll have to go now,' Jane told her.

Maggie headed for the wall phone at the quiet end of the corridor, then fretted with impatience as she waited for John's secretary to answer.

'Oh, is that you, Sarah? May I speak to John?'

'He's already left, I think—just a tick and I'll check.' More precious minutes down the drain; Maggie chewed at her lip. 'Missed him, I'm afraid.'

'Do you know where I could reach him?' Maggie asked anxiously.

'Some exhibition he was taking his parents to—where is anybody's guess. Nothing wrong, is there?'

'No, not really, the usual hospital goings-on. I'll leave a message on his answer-phone. If he should ring . . .'

'Yes, sure. We must all get together some time, Maggie.'

'Oh, yes, we must. Goodbye now—and thanks.'

Feeling rather at a loss, Maggie dialled John's home number. She loathed speaking into a tape, she came out sounding so diffident and unnatural when it was played back. But she put all the feeling into it she could, suspecting she was sounding like a third-rate movie. She hung up with relief and turned away from the phone as Paula Crisp emerged from her office wearing a pale blue pants suit. Seeing Maggie, Paula stopped to do a full turn.

'New theatre togs. What do you think?'

Maggie studied the cotton top and trim-fitting trousers with ill-concealed impatience—Jane would be frantic by now. 'Heavens,' she commented, 'they look far too good for us. Are the trousers comfortable?' she asked politely, suddenly conscious of whom she was talking to.

The Theatre Supervisor wrinkled her nose and plucked at the material around her hips. 'Could be a bit looser,' she admitted. She sighed. 'The dresses we wear might look dreary, but at least they go around everyone. Oh, Maggie, before I forget, you're doing this case this evening, aren't you? Don't forget to fill in the overtime forms. Now, I must go and see the housekeeper about these outfits. I'd hate to order several gross and find they wash into rags!'

It wouldn't be anything new if they did, Maggie could not help thinking. Jane was in the utility room, tongue between her teeth, carefully pouring formaldehyde over specimens in a jar. 'Don't tell me,' she said, not daring to look up least she spill a drop. 'You went into the City to see him. What did he say?'

'Sorry, I'd have taken a cab if I knew you were going to be touchy. No, seriously, I couldn't reach him and I had to leave a message on that infernal machine of his.'

'It'll be all right,' Jane soothed, but Maggie's eyes were grave.

'This time, somehow, I don't think it's going to be,' she said.

At exactly five o'clock Beth Liddell was pushed into the anaesthetic room. Maggie was busy checking back on some anaesthesia details from the previous operation, but she looked up with a smile, and as soon as the room had cleared of extraneous personnel went over to the bed. Beth was lying very quietly, all the natural colour had left her face and it was drawn-looking and tired.

'Hello,' said Maggie, smiling. 'You probably won't remember me,' she said gently. The girl's eyes seemed to burn right through her, but she said nothing. Maggie took her hand and swallowed hard as the dry little fingers curled round her own.

'Don't be daft, Maggie,' Alan joked softly, as he joined her at the bedside. 'In that get-up, your own mother wouldn't recognise you!'

'Mine didn't,' claimed Bronwyn, coming forward and wrapping a blood pressure cuff around Beth's good arm. 'I went to see her before she had her op, and she never recognised me. I kept saying, Mum, Mum, it's me! Well, she couldn't believe it, she said I looked as if I was going to take a shower, or something. She thought we wore glam things, like they did in *Magnificent Obsession* —she was really disappointed!'

Alan raised his eyebrows. 'You're far too young to have even heard of that old film!' Listening to them, Maggie was full of admiration for the way they worked, their ordinary everyday talk lessening Beth's fears so that she was scarcely aware what they were doing.

'Clench your fist—good girl! Now a prick, it won't hurt, soon be over . . .' Beth nodded sleepily. Maggie held her hand until she felt it go limp. Carefully she positioned it out of harm's way; for a moment she stood watching, then signalling that she was going, slipped quietly from the room, passing into the brilliantly lit theatre on her way to the scrub room.

Philip Lonsdale had already started. Maggie glanced up at the wall clock, making a mental note of the time before taking her place at the next empty sink to his. 'Seen Beth Liddell?' he asked, his voice brusque, and Maggie nodded, applying the liquid soap to her hands with a touch of her elbow. He shot her a sideways look. 'How does she seem to you?' he asked, noting the pale, set expression.

'She looked very frail, I thought,' said Maggie in a low voice.

'Hmm. You should take a look at the X-rays, then you'll know what frail means. That leg is going to be a bastard. I was hoping to get away with a femoropopliteal bypass, but I think I'll end up doing a long bypass right to the ankle. Got the full range out?'

Maggie nodded. She had every size of graft they possessed on the supplies table. Her head was bent and Philip wondered if she was being moody about having missed her night out. He wondered, too, who she was seeing.

If he had but known, that was the last thing on Maggie's mind; she was thinking about Beth. Some quality in the girl's small, heart-shaped face had touched her. 'She has a beautiful face,' Maggie said suddenly, her voice scarcely audible. 'Yesterday it was beautiful,' she amended. 'Today she seems wasted, already burnt up.' There was a definite tremor in her voice, and Philip gave her a strange look. Beth was worrying the hell out of him as it was, and at the beginning of a long and exhausting operation he did not need his nurse getting emotional. It led to all kinds of problems, not least diminished concentration.

Maggie scrubbed at her arms. 'She looked as if she couldn't take the sort of operation you're describing.'

Every surgeon lived with the nightmare of having a patient die under his knife. Philip was no exception, but at this point he could not allow himself to think of it. His face was stony. 'Leave the theatre before you start cultivating your emotions,' he said harshly, his arm grazing against hers.

Maggie felt the warm toughness of his bare skin with a pinprick of shock, but Philip seemed not to have noticed. He slammed the tap off with his elbow and reached for a towel. 'Either it's a long operation to save her leg, or a quick amputation—not much of a choice, you would agree. I think we should at least try.' His voice was gritty and tight; he was taking an awful risk and he knew it, Maggie knew it, and as the doors pushed open and Gary hurried in, he snarled, 'You're late, Dr MacDonald.'

The young house surgeon did not waste time denying it, but headed for the sink. When Lonsdale was in this sort of mood, you didn't argue.

'Get a central venous line-up?' Philip asked, and Gary nodded.

'Foley catheter?'

Gary's eyes jumped nervously to Maggie. 'The nurses put one in, didn't they?' He sounded dubious.

Philip ignored Maggie's affirmative and said, 'For God's sake, MacDonald, it's your job to check these things!' He threw his towel down and heaved into his gown, and as Jane hurried to do the ties, a leaden silence descended on them. As soon as he had gone, Gary, turned an enquiring eye on Maggie. 'What's eating him?' he wanted to know.

Maggie glanced up, leaping instantly to Philip's defence. 'He's worried sick,' she snapped, furious at the smug houseman. 'You've never had a patient die on the table—a patient, Gary, not an inanimate object under sterile green cloths!' She swallowed; her gown was suffocatingly hot, her neck prickled with embarrassment. Jane tied the tapes in a reproachful silence that added to her growing discomfort, more so even than Gary's long low whistle. How stupid of her to indulge in a remark like that! Stupid and thoughtless. With a prickle of anxiety she wondered if she was losing control —it happened sometimes, a nurse cracked. Maggie took a long breath. 'Sorry, I should never have said that.'

'Being Sister in Charge means never having to say sorry. You ever heard the Kaiser saying sorry?' Gary shook his head. 'Take a leaf out of her book and you'll rise to the top fast.'

Maggie laughed, she couldn't help it, and felt the better for it. The middle-aged Sister who ran Theatre Two had a reputation equal to none. Stories literally had her in jackboots, and were of course grossly exaggerated —however, medical students and house surgeons trod very warily on her ground.

'Give her enough time,' said Jane. 'Now would Sister like to do the count before H.E. comes back to see what the hell we're up to?'

'Ready?' Philip watched, his eyes shrewd over the mask as Maggie coiled the rubber suction hosing into a neat circle and pinned it carefully to the drapes. Unruffled, she laid out four Kelly's, scissors, and two small gauze squares. Only then did she affix the number four blade to the number four knife handle. Fiona had trained her nurses well: she was of the 'Be ready first' school of thought. 'Let a surgeon get his hands on the knife, he's through the skin and screaming for the Kellys before his nurse is halfway set up,' she always said.

'Ready,' Maggie said quietly, laying down the scalpel, her clear grey eyes lifting to his face. She had regained her equilibrium, and it showed; he acknowledged the fact with a flicker of his black lashes. As was his custom, he looked once at his patient's face, then he took up the scalpel and made his incision with a clean swift stroke.

By nine-thirty they were midway through the operation, Philip with one knee on a stool to ease the strain on his back. Gary was more at liberty to shift his position and was not required to maintain the same level of concentration, his main tasks being to snip and tie and try to keep abreast with what Philip was doing and answer questions more or less intelligently. Alan Bradford was reading his *BMJ*. Occasionally he twiddled a few knobs and made recordings, but despite the relaxed appearance, nothing, but nothing, escaped his notice; he had the best ear Maggie knew for discerning changes in respiratory patterns, and a sixth sense for trouble that had saved many a surgeon's reputation.

Jane and Sue had been replaced by the one-to-nine team, who were also on call for late work, and these in turn had been rotated off for twenty-minute coffee breaks. Although Beth was holding her own, her critical condition worried Philip so much he refused to take a break for himself. He pressed on, the insides of his gloves gummy with sweat and a slow spreading fire in his back from an old injury. He paused a moment to shift his position in an effort to relieve his cramped muscles. Maggie's tables, with the stacked pads, compresses, gauze squares, and the score of other items, looked as neat as when they started, her instruments marshalled in order with a precision that constantly astonished him. Lord knew how she managed it. His eyes swept over Maggie's face, noting the pallor with a twinge of conscience. Neither had she taken a break. He caught her eye. 'I'd suggest two orange and glucose with straws to go.' He smiled behind his mask, his eyes making fun of her.

'On the rocks?' she asked, perfectly serious.

'Please.'

'I'll call down for room service, sir.'

Philip laughed softly; it was a joke between them. The orange drinks were ready for them on a tray. One of the nurses would untie their masks and hold the glasses while they drank from straws.

At last it was finished, and Philip stepped away from the table. He dragged the mask from his face, breaking the strings, and flung it with his gloves into a discard bucket. He stayed for a quiet word with Alan, then with a word of thanks to them all, went to see Beth's parents who, despite the lateness of the hour, were waiting in her room.

'Rather him than me,' Gary said moodily.

'Why?' asked Maggie, as she bandaged. 'Hold the foot up, please, Gary. The operation's gone well, hasn't it? The toes are a good colour.' She paused with her bandaging, looking up. Gary shrugged.

'Well, let's hope,' he mumbled.

A chill touched Maggie. The operation had to work, it had to! The suction gargled and hissed as Alan cleared Beth's throat. She said carefully, 'The graft will work, I know it.'

The others had already gone by the time Maggie finally got along to the changing room and dragged herself through the ritual of getting dressed in outdoor clothing. A few more hours and she would be back again. Another day, another long list—she wondered how a surgeon could keep it up, year after year.

On the way to the front door, footsteps overtook her in the deserted corridor, and she looked up as Philip loomed alongside to fall in step with her. 'Have you transport?' he asked.

Maggie shook her head. 'No,' she said, but with a funny little catch of breath, 'I'm only five minutes away.'

Reaching the front doors, he stepped ahead to open them, and immediately they were caught in a cold gust of wind. Maggie jammed her uniform hat more securely on her head and pulled her coat collar up. She was very conscious of him beside her as they walked together towards the entrance. 'Come along, I'll give you a lift,' he said.

Maggie looked up between flying strands of hair, her eyes watering in the raw wind. 'Really, there's no need.' Her legs felt remarkably unsteady at the prospect. 'Thanks all the same,' she smiled, stepping away. There was a shout as a cyclist turned in at the hospital gates and she was pulled back from its path.

The cyclist wobbled to a stop a few yards further on and yelled back, 'You OK?'

Hard against Philip, with his arms still unaccountably around her, Maggie could not find the breath to reply. It was Philip who answered. 'She's fine, young man, but you get yourself a light or there'll be a serious accident!' He glanced down at her, his voice softening. 'And as for you . . . no more nonsense about walking home at this time of night!' Maggie surrendered meekly to his enforcing hand as she was led towards the medical staff car park where there were still a few cars in the bays. Philip stopped by a BMW and unlocked the door for her to get in.

Maggie slid gratefully into the seat. 'It's very kind of you,' she said, feeling ridiculously nervous as he reversed and headed on to the Fulham Road. 'Two streets along to the left,' she murmured.

They reached the street in two minutes, though to Maggie, sitting in dumb silence, it seemed longer. 'Just here will be fine,' she muttered, as they came abreast of the house, the only one on the quiet street that was ablaze with lights. Philip stopped the car and got out before she could protest. And then the unthinkable happened. The front door of the house opened to spill out a noisy group, Nigel in the forefront. Maggie shrank back, but it was too late, he had seen her.

'Darling!' he exclaimed, his exaggerated voice making her wince. 'We'd quite given you up, my sweet!'

Maggie viewed his flushed, excited appearance with anxious dismay. She was used to his flamboyant ways, but not Philip, whose expression had darkened. Some girls in shiny evening dresses, fur coats carelessly draped on bare shoulders, drifted down the steps after Nigel. They converged on Philip, all smiles. 'Nigel,' purred one, 'ask your handsome friend to come on to Clowns with us.'

Maggie groaned inwardly at the mention of the notorious nightclub Nigel frequented. But worse was to come as Nigel's voice fell on her horrified ears. 'Put on something divine, sweetie, and let's go.'

Nigel was always urging her to go out with him, but of course she never took his proposals seriously. Philip had, she saw that instantly. The look he threw her was steely. 'Party all you want, but I'll be on my way,' he said curtly.

There were disappointed cries from the girls. An effeminate young man Maggie had not noticed before flipped the end of a white silk scarf over one shoulder, saying to Philip, 'My, my, are you the cool one!'

Maggie could have died.

As Philip got into his car without a backward glance, she slipped from the group and ran for the front steps. Chewing at her lip, she paused just inside the front door to watch his car disappear up the street. Confused at how depressed that made her, she turned away. There was a hand-delivered envelope waiting for her on the front table, addressed in John's handwriting. Snatching it up, she took the stairs two at a time. Once inside her room, she leaned her back against the door, listening with closed eyes as Nigel's sports car came to life with a full-throttled roar. When silence had settled once again she switched on the light and looked at the envelope in her hand.

CHAPTER THREE

WITH trembling fingers Maggie smoothed out the folds in the stiff notepaper. 'Dear Margaret,' the letter began disquietingly. This made Maggie pause right at the beginning, for John never addressed her as such, and her eyes scanned the next words anxiously. 'Did it occur to you, I wonder—when you decided your obligation to the hospital was infinitely more important than your commitment to me—how much you would disappoint my parents, who had only the one evening to spend in London, or that it might not cause me embarrassment having to explain your absence?' Maggie felt herself recoiling from the sharp words, but she read on. 'And if so, then surely you must now admit that we've reached a point in our relationship when you should consider giving up these ridiculous hours and think about taking a nine-to-five job . . .'

There was more, but Maggie's eyes travelled swiftly to the end, to read the one cold, flat word at the bottom: 'John'. No mention of love, no words that might help mitigate her guilt. Maggie read the letter through time and again, and when finally she did drop into an exhausted sleep, it came as a shock to have Jane shake her awake and to find that she had overslept the alarm by as much as an hour.

'Lord, I forgot you were on late shift today,' muttered Maggie, ignoring a proffered mug of coffee as she leapt from the bed in a panic, feeling sick. While Jane pulled the curtains she searched wildly for something to wear, then in desperation, she dragged a pair of jeans from the pile of unironed laundry, promising herself she would come straight home that evening and do all the things she'd had so little time for, like ironing and tidying . . .

Jane hovered by with the coffee, but Maggie shook her head. 'Thanks all the same, but I haven't time. Be a dear and phone them for me, ask Pat Mudie to start getting scrubbed. She'll have to assist in my place now that I'm late. We've got that big bone graft case first on the list.'

'I'll phone straight away,' promised Jane, but she still lingered, her eyes on Maggie's pinched face. 'You look awful!'

'I feel awful,' Maggie admitted, and rubbed her eyes which felt curiously dry and gritty. 'Let's hope I'm not coming down with the 'flu—it would be the last straw. I felt quite odd last night—and John's letter didn't help any, I felt bad enough as it was, thinking I'd let him down and disappointed his parents. And that's another thing —I wanted to be up early, so I could phone them and apologise before they left this morning. I'll write to them, of course.' So saying, she picked up a brush and scraped it through a tangle of curls. A quick look in the mirror and she decided she looked as miserable as she felt.

'You know,' she told Jane, 'he's insisting that I get a nine-to-five job, with weekends, and holidays like normal people.' She stared moodily at her reflection. A few weeks back she had been full of confidence for the future—her future and John's. But suddenly, bleakly, that had all changed. She threw down the brush. 'I should worry, I won't have a blessed job if I don't get a move on! You know what Lonsdale's like about punctuality.'

Already gowned and gloved when she arrived, Philip summed up the dark circles and pale face in one shrewd glance. After leaving her the night before, he had wondered if she would go on and make a night of it, and it was patently obvious now that she had. Probably been out all night, he surmised, and his lips tightened. Well, the hell with it if she thought she could get away with those kind of hours!

Maggie braced herself against the angry look, hesitating just inside the scrub room door to tie her mask strings securely on top of her cap. Philip's dark eyes swept over her slender form, the upstretched arms and taut rounded

ON CALL IN THEATRE

breasts undermining years of discipline, leaving his senses sharp with desire. Thoroughly unsettled, he turned abruptly away, furious with himself for allowing this lapse in his concentration. He snapped, 'Don't hurry on our account, Sister Bell.'

Maggie's eyes sparked. They warned that, late though she was, she wasn't prepared to put up with any snide remarks. Ignoring Duncan's clammy look of sympathy, she stalked through to the middle room where Pat Mudie was scrubbed and ready, placidly arming her needle-holders.

When the instrument count had been taken, the morning got under way with the usual mad rush to get the surgical team set up and the patient positioned as required, for a complicated surgical manoeuvre that involved two different operation sites. When at last the theatre was humming smoothly, Maggie was able to settle back a little and clear her mind. But it soon became apparent that Philip was getting more and more irritated. Pat was lagging behind him and becoming flustered, and so eventually, when his patience ran out with the chisel he was using, he swore silently and threw it back on the table. 'That thing's so blunt, it wouldn't cut through butter! Get it sharpened.'

Maggie's eyes went to the orthopaedic table, then back to him. 'They have been, sir,' she said calmly, for she had seen to it personally and the set had been returned the evening before.

'Then go and get the person responsible and let him try and chip his way through bone,' said Philip, but with a touch of dry humour in his voice, and he accepted the next in size that Pat handed him without further comment. There was an unknown quantity to Maggie that stopped him from pushing her too far. For all he knew, she might just go and ring for the man.

The case took longer and was even more complicated than ever Maggie had thought, and it was almost one o'clock when they wheeled the patient down to Recovery. Although it was lunchtime, she had yet to finish setting up for the afternoon list, so telling the others to go on, she made do with a cup of coffee from the common room. Her stomach felt empty, but she wasn't in the least hungry. Indeed, the very thought of food made her feel queasy, which wasn't like her at all.

With the staff on lunch break, she had the big storeroom to herself, and she was so absorbed in getting a list of requirements from the racks that she never noticed Philip enter the room until he was right behind her.

'Not going to lunch, Sister?' Maggie spun round and found his blue eyes on her in a hard stare. 'I suppose you think you can do without food as well.'

She looked straight back at him, so nonplussed he felt constrained to explain himself. 'As well as sleep,' he muttered, unaccountably irritated to find the level gaze had not altered in its disconcerting intensity.

'Sleep? Oh . . .' Maggie thought of the hours she had spent mulling over John's letter. 'I didn't get much,' she admitted somewhat ruefully, her eyes at last dropping to the top button of his white coat.

His mouth twisted. 'I can imagine.' And something in the tone of his voice jerked Maggie's eyes back to his face. 'What you do with your free time is your business,' he snapped, 'but if your social activities leave you so tired you can't get your mind on your job . . .'

Maggie looked at him, outraged. 'The hours I spend in this job,' she flashed back at him, 'there's precious little time for social activities!'

'Then find one that will,' he snarled, driven out of his aloofness and into an uncharacteristic remark by this slip of a girl who didn't quite come up to his shoulders. She stood looking up at him with those eyes of lambent silver—pale and shadowy under the neon lights—and he saw she was trembling. A quite unreasonable anger took hold of him. 'Look at you!' he exploded. 'How long do you think you can get away with burning the candle at both ends?'

Maggie's cheeks burned with resentment. It wasn't often she had a sleepless night—and she wasn't going to let him bully her just because she had the temerity to look tired on duty. 'If you have any complaints about my work, then please say,' she said coldly, lifting her chin to meet his angry look full on.

'Who did the specimens this morning?' But it was an accusation, not a question, and Maggie's heart sank. She'd had to leave the theatre for a few moments to phone an important message through to the pathologist —Sue had taken the two chips of bone from Pat, one from the diseased part, and one from healthy tissue. A look into the cold blue eyes and Maggie knew the specimens had been muddled.

Philip was watching her carefully. Maggie knew as well as he how vitally important the laboratory specimens were, and for all her tiredness, he couldn't really believe she had been so careless. The strained mouth told him she must know how it had happened, though.

The last thing Maggie wanted was for Sue's name to come up yet again. In any case, she felt that the ultimate responsibility belonged to her as Theatre Sister. She was where the buck stopped. It simply meant she would have to go over the procedure of collecting specimens again, and again and again, if necessary, until everybody knew it off by heart.

As her silence persisted, Philip dismissed it with an angry shrug. 'As it happened, I noticed they'd been incorrectly labelled before they went to Pathology.'

'Oh, thank God!' Maggie exclaimed, feeling light-headed with relief. 'So that's all right, then.'

'No!' he said, the vehemence in his voice making her wince. 'It's far from all right, as you say. It may have cost that man another trip to theatre for a bone biopsy . . .' He stopped, his eyes sweeping over her. She had no right to look so dead tired, and at the same time so outrageously beautiful. Something in her fragile little face made him want to crush her protectively in his arms.

Maggie was beginning to feel dreadfully unwell and she gave her head a tiny shake in an effort to clear it. 'I understand that,' she told him, 'and it won't happen again.' Desperately hoping that would be an end to the matter, and he would go and let her get on while there was still a chance of her finishing what she had begun, she turned away and seized an autoclaved crate, the next item that happened to be on her list. As she did, a pain clenched her stomach into a knot and sent her spinning into inky blackness.

Then, the next thing, she was cradled in powerful arms, safe and secure, and the pain had become a dark tangled memory. Her legs were incapable of supporting her, but it seemed not to matter.

'Maggie, for God's sake look at me!' Her eyelids were heavy; it seemed to take an enormous effort to open them. And then she was looking into eyes so gentle and so tender, it was the most natural thing in the world to slide her arms up and around his neck, and nestle her head deep in his broad shoulder, away from the strong neon lights which bothered her and caused her eyes to hurt.

Philip caught his breath agonisingly in his throat as he felt the exquisite softness of her body. Gently he pulled the tight cap from her hair. It was thick and warm to the touch, and he buried his face in its bright, sweet-smelling richness. In the thin dress she felt naked against him, the silkiness of her skin a torment. Unthinking, Maggie raised her face to him, soft lips that held a hint of voluptuousness, and he locked her hard to him with a strong surge of possessiveness.

The feel of her was like a sudden raging fever, and the need he had denied for so long exploded, and he surrendered with a low pained cry, beginning to kiss her face ravenously, sinking deeper and deeper into his passion, his hands feverish and hungry for her.

In another moment he would have succumbed, and lost the age-old battle against will. Philip lifted his head and stood motionless, sucking in long breaths. He stood for long moments fighting for control, his breath ragged, his arms wrapped tightly around her.

Maggie, vulnerable and melting in his arms, slipped through a dream world where time and place held no meaning, and no longer sure where she ended and he began. She had ceased to be a separate entity. It was a glorious floaty feeling.

'Maggie . . . Maggie . . .' His voice was urgent now, and she made an attempt to respond, then the pain was back, wrenching her insides apart. White-lipped, she moaned. Philip picked her up, as light as a feather, her head against his shoulder, and carried her out and along the corridor to the intensive care unit.

Maggie heard the murmur of voices as he shouldered his way through the swing doors, then she was carefully lowered on to a bed as though she were a fragile piece of china, and a nurse was pulling the screens. Philip was saying something in a quiet voice and the nurse hurried away. Maggie held herself tight as the pain came ripping its way through her abdomen, biting her lip until it hurt, then Philip was by her side again.

'Let's take a look.' Deftly he drew her dress up, exposing her bare slender legs and the skimpy panties she had on. Maggie was aware of nothing but the pain and the touch of his hands gently prodding and palpating in a thorough examination of her abdominal area.

'Tell me where it hurts, Maggie?' he asked, his voice gentle and coaxing. Despite the discomfort, her heart leapt at the way he had said her name.

'All over,' she gasped, turning her head away. Had she walked here, or had he carried her? She wasn't quite certain.

'Appendix out?' he asked, and she shook her head miserably, eyes tight shut as he persisted with his questions.

'How long have you been feeling unwell?' And she answered, 'Only this morning when I got up,' and then heard his 'Ahh . . .!' as if it was something that didn't surprise him. As if it was the morning after the night before, and perhaps she could expect to be feeling unwell. Maggie kept her face turned to the wall, too ill to think up a defensive reply, then the nurse was back.

Philip's voice hardened a little as he told her what he was going to do, and before she could protest the nurse was helping her into a sitting position and rolling her dress up so Philip could examine her lungs with his stethoscope. Being so rushed for time that morning, she hadn't bothered to search for a clean bra, so she was wearing nothing at all. Red with embarrassment, she coughed obediently and breathed in and out as he commanded.

When it was over, he let her lie back. His face was inscrutable as he pressed his stethoscope to the left of her breastbone to record the apex beat. Her eyes flew open, panic and simultaneous excitement sweeping through her when his long powerful fingers brought a telling response; Philip carefully avoided looking into those wide grey eyes, for he was more shaken by the effect she was having on him than he cared to admit. It took all his will-power just to maintain a cool professional profile. He couldn't think what had got into him, but he was certain it would pass.

'Right,' he said, a moment later, as relieved as she was that it was over. 'Get Sister Bell into a hospital gown, please, nurse.'

Slowly the realisation sank in that she might be staying. That was ridiculous! The pain had gone and her head was quite clear again. She had to get back to work. 'Oh, please,' she implored, 'it's nothing . . .'

'Maggie . . .' He spoke to her as if she might have been a child, as he sat down on the bed, taking her hand in his. 'It's anything but. I don't think you have appendicitis either, but I want you to stay here for a few hours while we run some tests. Going back to work is out of the question for the time being.'

She stared at him. 'I'm just tired, that's all,' she began, then stopped, realising by the hard shuttered look on his face that she had said the wrong thing.

'Perhaps you might like to consider my advice to you earlier, and get a few early nights,' said Philip acidly, standing up as the nurse came back with a gown and a pile of other things Maggie didn't care to think about; she had a good healthy dread of being a patient herself, in hospital.

'I'll be back to see you later,' he told her formally, and the curtains fluttered behind his broad back as he strode out of the cubicle. The nurse, whose eyes had also followed him out, turned back to Maggie.

'You lucky thing! I wouldn't mind being carried in here by Philip Lonsdale—how did you manage it?'

'I fainted,' Maggie mumbled, suddenly acutely embarrassed when she thought how that sounded, especially when the nurse trilled, 'I would too, if he was there to catch me! Arms up, love.' Faintly resentful, Maggie slipped into the gown and allowed herself to be settled against the pillows. She felt too weak to object, and after the nurse had gone, her lids dropped like stones, though she could hear quite clearly what was being said on the other side of the curtains.

'Would you believe, right into his arms! My God, some people have all the luck . . .' And then the murmuring got lower and lower and lower . . .

'What's all this, then?'

Maggie opened her eyes, surprised to find she had been sound asleep, because the nurse was back with a doctor whom she recognised to be the senior consultant physician, Dr Gerald Ryder. He was leaning over the bed proffering a benign smile. Maggie only wished she could go back to sleep, but she answered all his questions and subjected herself to another examination. At last he pronounced himself satisfied, assured her she wasn't going down with anything too serious and went on his way.

The next face belonged to a young man with spiky hair and a white coat several sizes too large for him. He was hovering by her bed with a box of syringes and glass tubes. 'Won't be a jiff,' he said pleasantly, and produced a tourniquet. Maggie guessed he was here to take blood off and closed her eyes, quite prepared to ignore the whole procedure. 'This won't hurt,' the young man told her.

Maggie felt a prick and she opened her eyes, watching uninterestedly as the syringe slowly filled with blood. Quite without warning, her stomach heaved, she gasped, 'I'm going to be sick,' and he was shouting for a bowl.

The bowl duly arrived and Maggie sat hunched over it for a few minutes, but the feeling had worn off and she lay back, exhausted.

'Don't worry,' grinned the doctor with infuriating cheerfulness, 'blood often affects people like that.'

'It might,' the nurse said, giving him a level look, 'but not often to Theatre Sisters.

She was ignored and Maggie was favoured with another cheeky grin. 'You don't look old enough.'

Then it was temperature and pulse time again, and all desire for sleep had passed. Maggie was beginning to feel a bit foolish, lying on a bed in the unit. Had she really fainted? Thinking about it, she blushed to the roots of her hair. Perhaps she had imagined it. Difficult to tell when her body ached, and she felt feverish, and it was all mixed up with a hot, strange, empty feeling in the pit of her stomach.

The curtains parted and Philip's dark head appeared. 'Ah, you're awake.' Her eyes slid nervously away from his face, her mouth was so dry it made speaking impossible, and she was trembling. Maybe she hadn't imagined the feel of that long hard body, or his wild passionate kisses.

'Still feeling nauseated?' She nodded, and he said something to the attentive nurse by his side and Maggie was quick to notice the deliberate flutter of eyelashes as she handed him the treatment chart. 'Stemitil IM stat,' he said, writing down the order and handing the chart back. Another flutter of lashes – oh, really! thought Maggie; not that she cared, of course, she reminded herself quickly. Anyway, Philip Lonsdale never noticed how the nurses looked at him.

'Looks as if you might have some kind of virus,' he told her. In his immaculate white coat and grey worsted suit he looked so professional it was difficult to think she had melted into his arms, and she blushed again. Noting the high colour, Philip reached for the temperature chart and looked at the line spiking above normal. 'Hmm . . .

How would you feel about spending a few days in Women's Medical, if it can be arranged?'

Maggie couldn't think of anything worse. 'No,' she croaked. 'If it's only a virus I'd rather go home.' She managed a weak laugh. 'Heavens, I'd never be able to get any rest in here.'

'On the contrary,' he said, 'you'd probably get a lot more. However . . .' he shrugged, and his dark blue eyes made it perfectly clear that it didn't really concern him one way or the other, if she wanted to be silly. 'The chief says you can go if you want, it's up to you. So long as you rest up for the next week.'

'A week!' exclaimed Maggie in disbelief. How could she get a week off when they were short-staffed and pushed to the limit as it was? 'It's not possible,' she said, as crisply as she could, which was difficult lying on her back in bed while he towered over her.

'No one is indispensable,' he said, a soft teasing note she hated in his voice. 'I'll pick you up at seven and drive you home.' He waved aside her protests, then smiled his goodbyes and left, the nurse at his heels.

'Oh,' Maggie said soundlessly, and stared at the ceiling. She felt terribly at odds with herself, rather as if she needed a good shoulder to cry on. She thought of John, and only succeeded in making herself more miserable. She was hot and her throat hurt. Then she got impatient; she had the 'flu, nothing more and nothing less, so she could expect to feel miserable. It was true, nurses made the worst patients.

After the injection she dropped into a heavy drug-induced sleep. Once she half woke, and thought she could hear a girl crying. Was it Beth? she wondered, unable to wake properly before drifting back to sleep again; only this time to uneasy dreams peopled with half-remembered figures, and always, running through them, was this deep sad longing.

The next time she woke, Philip was there. Maggie's thoughts flew in all directions. How long had he been standing by her bed? Was her hair in an awful mess, and her face plain without any make-up? To his polite enquiry as to how she was feeling, she answered quickly, 'Better, thanks.'

'You don't look it. But if you still want to go home, I'm here to take you.' He glanced at her from under his black brows, taking in the too pale skin and the shadows under her eyes. By the evasive look that crossed her face, he wondered impatiently if there was someone else she would have preferred to come and pick her up.

What had she let herself in for? Maggie was thinking. For now that he was standing before her in the flesh, it suddenly dawned on her that he would take her home and find the place a mess. Nigel was sure to be there with half a dozen of his friends, and that hadn't worked out too well the last time Philip had driven her back. She groaned inwardly, but even as she was struggling to find some excuse that would get her out of it, he was organising the nurse into taking her to the front door in a chair. A chair? Oh hell . . . There would be no end of fiendishly funny stories once the wags got hold of that! But she had to accept it, and before he went she asked if she could see Beth.

'Certainly not. She doesn't need your virus,' he growled, having watched the lack of enthusiasm with considerable ire; he was, after all, putting himself out for her—then he felt like an ogre when he saw the expression in her grey eyes. For some reason it hurt right down to his soul. 'Beth is asleep,' he told her gruffly. 'She's comfortable at present, and I think it wise if we don't disturb her. Now stop worrying, because she's making a good post-op recovery.'

He sighed; he had never known a girl so quiet. It was almost as if she were doing him a favour, and not the other way round. He was almost relieved when the nurse came back with the chair. 'Five minutes,' he said with a brief smile, and departed.

As they waited at the front door for Philip to drive up with the car, Maggie noticed a woman standing by the reception desk. She was the sort of woman whose ice-cool looks drew a second glance. Maggie was covertly admiring the sleekly coiled hair, and wondering how it managed to stay so neat, when Philip walked through; she got up out of the chair gladly, thanking the nurse with a wry apologetic smile, then turned to discover the blonde woman hurrying forward to meet him. Philip greeted her as though they had been long acquainted; he barely glanced in Maggie's direction.

Maggie felt an ache of jealousy, as irrational as anything that had happened to her that day. And then Philip was bringing her over to be introduced. The woman couldn't take her eyes off him, Maggie noticed, and was so absurdly irritated by it she failed to catch the last name. Claudia somebody-or-other; what did she care?

She listened while Philip explained why Maggie was waiting for him—and no, he wasn't doing anything special that evening, and yes, he would be delighted to drive her round to look at the flat, he knew she was going to like it—he just had to drop Maggie off first.

He might have been speaking about a parcel, Maggie thought, more and more resentful, quite forgetting her earlier objections. Only too horribly conscious of her own dishevelled mop of curls and wan face, she stood on one foot and then another, looking at the cool classical features of this woman who commanded Philip Lonsdale's full attention, and she felt like the uninvited guest at a party.

At the car, Claudia slipped unhesitatingly into the front seat, leaving Maggie to get in the back. When they had all settled, she turned to Maggie with a small exclamation on her carefully outlined lips.

'Not the Sister Bell who's been filling in for Fiona?' And as Maggie slowly nodded, she turned back, a charming note of reproof in her voice. 'Philip, you might have said!'

His hand on the gear shift, Philip turned his head to meet Maggie's look of enquiry; reluctantly, she thought, as if he wasn't yet ready with an explanation.

'Claudia was my instrument nurse before she went to America,' he explained quietly. 'That was a few years ago.' He paused, and an expression crossed his face that made Maggie wonder what Claudia meant to him. 'Well, she's back now,' he went on, a slight smile for Claudia, 'and she wants to apply for Fiona's position.'

Maggie's mouth formed an 'Oh.' That was all. Nothing else, except for a look in her grey eyes that made him turn away and let out the clutch with an impatient jab. Why the hell did she have to go and break her heart over this job? There was time enough for her to grow old and frosty, as he was convinced all Theatre Sisters became eventually. Let women like Claudia—who might look like Dresden china but who in fact were genuine cast-iron—let them do it. They were able to cut it up rough without being hurt, damn it.

Later that evening Jane sat at the end of Maggie's bed in comfortable red woollen slippers and said gloomily, 'She was with Paula Crisp for ages this afternoon. People who remember her groan, I'm telling you! They say she's a maniac for tidiness.' Jane looked round the room. 'My God, and she came up here with you!'

Maggie gazed miserably at the mess. 'She insisted on seeing me up. I was about to die of shame. He stayed in the hall, thank goodness. I was petrified in case Nigel came rollicking in with his cronies.' With a short laugh, she added, 'Claudia didn't stay long. One good look and she beat it.'

'Be thankful for small mercies,' said Jane. 'Well, anyway, you look a whole lot better than you did this morning. A couple of days will do wonders for you—all right, a week. Make the most of it and lie about and read the glossies. I would.' She yawned and stretched.

Maggie pulled a face. 'Yes, while Claudia takes over, I suppose.' It sounded silly, but the thought of Claudia taking her place hurt much more than if it had been somebody else, like Pat, or Jane, or one of the others.

'Someone has to,' Jane pointed out. As if Maggie didn't know it. She had grown very quiet, and Jane was dying to ask how she came to fall into Philip Lonsdale's arms in a dead faint. No feminist, Maggie. But for one whose self-control was phenomenal, to say nothing of a formidable pride, it seemed about the unlikeliest thing Jane had ever heard of. Yet that was what that dilly of a nurse in the ITU swore had happened. However, it was no good trying to probe. Maggie could clam up—if there was something she didn't want to discuss, then nothing on God's earth could get it out of her. And this Jane knew better than anybody. She sighed. 'What are you going to do about John?' she asked.

'John?' Maggie echoed with a start, and a guilty flush swept her face; she had hardly spared him a thought. 'He should have phoned by now. Funny, isn't it, any other evening I would be worried if he hadn't called at his usual time, but tonight? Oh, I don't know, I've been feeling strange all day. Well, I guess I'll get over it.'

'What is it you think you're going to get over?' Jane asked slyly.

'Why, the 'flu, of course,' Maggie told her with a frown. 'And as to what I'm going to do—about John, his demands, or my job, I don't know. I haven't decided yet.'

And about Philip Lonsdale? Jane asked herself. Because she knew something about the man, and it wasn't often he acknowledged the existence of a nurse as another entity, let alone show any sign of possessiveness. And wasn't that what he had done by insisting on driving Maggie home from the hospital when any number of her friends would have seen her safely back—in a cab if necessary.

At first when Maggie had told her, she had had a wild desire to laugh, but now she wondered. Maggie was such an innocent. On the strength of today's happenings, anybody else would have been plotting to capture the man permanently. But not Maggie; there wasn't a devious thought in her head, apparently. What was more, she probably wouldn't give the episode any thought at all.

But there Jane was wrong. Maggie simply hid things too well. It was an old lesson well learned, a quality her father was proud of in her. After Jane had gone to bed the façade was allowed to drop, and she sat with hunched knees and despairing face. Her every instinct was to do as John wanted her, and yet . . . and yet . . .

But why not? Wasn't this a good a time as any to give up? Claudia would jump into her shoes, no doubt about that, especially when she had worked with Philip Lonsdale before. Maggie thumped the pillow and tried to get comfortable—the woman was tailor-made for the position. Strange, though, her turning up right at this moment, just as it became known that Fee would not be back—unless, of course, Philip had told her. That was it, probably, he had got in touch with her.

Once again she fell to wondering what Claudia meant to him. Was she really an old flame from the past? And then suddenly she was remembering the powerful feel of his body as she came to in his arms. He had kissed her, and she had kissed him back.

Oh God! She felt as if she had a raging fever. She threw back the covers and snatching up her robe padded restlessly down to the kitchen to make a pot of tea. The rest of the night she tossed and turned, only dropping off when the blackbird outside her window started calling his morning song.

Surprisingly she slept until early afternoon, and woke to find a thermos of hot coffee by her bedside and a bottle of spring water. Propped against it was a note reminding her to drink plenty of fluid; Jane also said she would be late again that night, so not to expect her home for tea. There was no message to say John had called.

For a while Maggie was content to sip her coffee and turn the pages of a magazine. It was strange being home when it wasn't her day off. She wondered who would have taken over that day. Well, she thought, remembering Philip's words to her, no one is indispensable. He was right, of course, and nowhere more than in Theatre where the turnover rate was so high. Why, people left, they just dropped out of sight and the work went on, and a week later everyone had practically forgotten their name. Unless it was someone like Fee who was sort of an institution.

The silence in the large empty house had begun to be oppressive. The cold outside turned the windows icy blue, and the day before seemed more of a fantasy than ever. If Philip had kissed her, it had obviously meant little to him, and she had been silly to lose so much sleep over it. Maggie made up her mind then and there not to think about it, or him.

But he stayed on in her memory like a small persistent pain, and finally a peculiar feeling of loneliness drove her downstairs, where she picked over the mail on the hall table. There was nothing for her, so she made her way disconsolately to the kitchen, opening the fridge and scowling at the neat row of eggs. The mere thought of food made her stomach lurch; she shut the door and made do with a little dry toast. After that she was only too happy to go back to bed, slide down beneath the covers and drift back to sleep.

Much later she woke to find it was quite dark, and someone was knocking on her door. She fumbled for the light switch. 'Come in,' she called, and was surprised when Nigel entered, carrying a basket tray which he deposited snugly across her knees. Maggie gazed at the bowl of soup on the tray and the neat little fingers of buttered toast, and felt hungry for the first time in days. 'Nigel, how lovely! Oh, you are thoughtful,' she smiled.

'Think nothing of it, ducky. How are you feeling?' He puckered up his lips. 'Nothing contagious?' His expression was so comic Maggie nearly burst out laughing, but she managed to keep a straight face because she knew Nigel took these things seriously, and assured him it was only a run-of-the-mill virus she had.

Nigel waved a hand. 'That I can take. You medical people make me so nervous. God knows what dreadful diseases you pick up at the hospital. I was fully expecting you to be a perfectly hideous yellow!'

This time Maggie did laugh. 'No, they checked me out for hepatitis. Don't worry, I'd be incarcerated in the hospital if it was anything serious. Thanks anyway for the soup, you are a dear.'

Now that the risks of fraternising seemed negligible, Nigel was quite prepared to sit down on her bed and gossip. He could be very amusing, and Maggie found it a relief to be drawn from her own chaotic thoughts. She sampled the soup as she listened, and pronounced it exquisite.

'Should be—it's my mum's special. She left us several jars when she came round yesterday.' He got up and wandered over to her dressing table, picking up a bottle of perfume and sniffing at the stopper; it was the one John had given her for Christmas.

'Sexy, exciting little number,' he said, in the confident voice of a connoisseur, and it swept over Maggie in that instant that those were the two elements missing in her relationship with John. Perhaps she had always unconsciously known. She had simply told herself often enough, other things were more important. But she knew in a blinding flash that they weren't. To be even more honest, she had known it yesterday, in Philip's arms. Her face burned so that she thought it must surely ignite. Fortunately Nigel's attention was focused elsewhere, and a moment later he dashed from the room.

He was back in no time. 'The perfect thing! Why didn't I think of it before?' and he dangled a slinky object in shimmering black lurex in front of Maggie's astonished eyes.

'Remember Liv? The girl with long blonde hair? She made it up and then the client changed her mind.' He hung the dress on her wardrobe. It was sleeveless and backless, and very sexy. 'Goes with your perfume,' he said, looking at it reflectively. 'What do you think?'

'I think it's beautiful, but I could never afford it.' What Maggie really meant was, she couldn't see herself ever going to any place she could wear it. Very faintly she heard the front door bell, but Nigel dismissed it. 'Bunny's downstairs, he'll answer it,' and Maggie vaguely wondered who Bunny was.

'I bought the damn thing,' Nigel admitted with surprising suddenness. 'I told Liv it was for my sister—I only did it to help her out. So here I am with a dress, and it would look better on you than me.'

That struck Maggie as particularly funny, and she rolled back on her pillows, almost breathless with mirth. Nigel came over and sat on the bed. 'You'd look smashing in it, Maggie, and you'd be doing me a favour if you took it off my hands. At least keep it in your wardrobe until you decide.'

Dear kind, generous Nigel! Maggie sat up, placing an impulsive hand on his arm. 'Nigel, that's really sweet of you. I don't know though—you see, I couldn't really imagine wearing something like that.'

'You should,' he told her, quite seriously. 'And Liv would be relieved to think someone with your figure was wearing her creation. She's seen my sister, and believe me . . . !' He gave a sudden grin.

Maggie smiled. 'Well, thanks, let me think about it.' She paused. 'You like Liv a lot, don't you?'

'Like her?' His voice broke. 'Maggie, I love the girl.' Then to her surprise, he suddenly leaned over and planted an affectionate kiss on her cheek. As he drew back, a deliberate cough came from the open door; startled, they both turned their heads at once.

Philip stood in the doorway, dark hair windblown and long lean body taut as whipcord. Maggie could guess what he must be thinking and she stared at him glassy-eyed with embarrassment. Snatching her hand from Nigel's arm, she dragged the sheet to her chin and said the first inane thing that came into her head. 'You two have met, I think?'

Philip directed a cursory nod at Nigel, who Maggie noticed in an agonised glance managed to look both guilty and uninterested at the same time. An awful silence enveloped the three of them.

'It's all right, I'm not staying,' Philip said at last, in the kind of voice that people use when they have inadvertently interrupted an intimate moment, and at a small protest from Maggie he added, 'I was passing, so I dropped in to see how you were making out . . .' The unfortunate phrase hung stickily in the air, and Philip cursed under his breath for his slip of tongue. 'Anyway . . .' Diffidently, as if already regretting the sudden impulse which had prompted a stop at the florist, he produced a cone of crisply wrapped daffodils from behind his back. 'I thought you might like these.'

While Maggie gazed at the flowers, Nigel recovered some of his old aplomb. 'Listen, ducky, I'll hunt up something to put them in. Then I'm off—Bunny managed tickets for a show tonight.' When he had slid from the room, Maggie pulled the sheet even higher, peering over the top and emitting a kind of watery laugh. 'Goodness alone knows who Bunny is!'

Philip flipped her a look that conveyed more adequately than words his thoughts about the household she had chosen to live in, and muttered unkindly, 'He's the camp character with the white silk scarf,' and then as he saw how white her face was, felt sorry he had said it. Somewhat abashed, he glanced about the room.

Claudia had obviously exaggerated when she had compared it to a chicken coop. Admittedly it was on the small side, and crammed to bursting with possessions —but there was something endearing and very feminine about the collection of colourful scarves, the chipped pieces of fine china filled with dried flowers, and the photographs—which he noticed almost obliterated the small oval mirror on her dresser. Maggie wondered if he was looking for a place to sit, and glanced at the chair with its load of clothes.

'Dump those things on the floor, if you want . . .' She had managed to make it sound as if she was entirely uninterested whether he went or stayed, but her large eyes, peering anxiously over the top sheet, could not have been more compelling. Almost against his will, Philip found he was bestowing a boyish grin on her and seating himself at the foot of the bed. The air was sluiced with the fresh green-bitter scent, and he remembered the daffodils he still held in his hands.

'Oh, they're wonderful,' Maggie said softly, emerging from the covers and reaching out her arms to take them.

'You look wonderful,' Philip said, and amended quickly, as if he had made a tactical error, 'You look as if you'd had some sleep.' The truth was, he had the greatest of difficulty in lifting his eyes from Maggie's satiny shoulders; did she really think that slip of crêpe-de-Chine she was wearing passed for a nightdress?

It was unthinkable, ludicrous, but he had a violent urge to take her in his arms and kiss her fiercely—and had to remind himself that his visit was professional. Momentarily he wondered if he had been working too hard.

What should she do, Maggie panicked, ask him if he would like a cup of tea? And if he accepted, how could she get out of bed and into her dressing gown, which in any case he was sitting on. Oh, where was Nigel? Before she could decide what was for the best, Philip had settled his long legs into a comfortable position and was enquiring about her health in the manner of a family doctor.

'No need to tell you how concerned we all are,' he was telling her smoothly, 'or the importance of getting yourself quite well again before coming back to work. Paula has checked on your sick leave—you have quite a lot accumulated, apparently.' Maggie remained silent. He sounded rather too glib, and she had a sudden prickly feeling that his concern was more to do with politics and smoothing the way for Claudia than it had to do with her health. Unconsciously she clenched her hands, and the stiff wrapping paper beneath them crackled in protest. Philip, glancing down, noticed the diamond ring on her finger, and slowly his eyes returned to her face. 'I didn't know you were engaged?' The shock in his voice was palpable.

Maggie stared at him, as if seeing the small details of his face for the first time: the lines traced in by worry and care, the lines of humour around his mouth and eyes. Suppose she were to tell him? Her heart thundered, then dulled. Tell him what? That she had suddenly decided not to be engaged? Slip the ring off with a casual laugh and say she had fallen out of love with her fiancé?

'Well, I expect you'll be getting married soon . . .' And Maggie saw in a flash the futility of saying anything. The one thing she wanted to discuss with him was the one thing she could not. Taking her silence to be an affirmative, Philip said, 'I see.'

Maggie flinched at the cold distant tone. She had been right, hadn't she? He would never understand, and how could she explain, if she didn't know herself when the decision to break her engagement with John had formed in her mind? Though she suspected it had been lying dormant there quite some while.

He smiled grimly. 'Once you're a married woman your job won't be so important to you.'

Important? Maggie blinked. 'Of course it is!' she protested, startled that this was what he should think. 'When a man marries, it makes no difference to his job, so why should it for a woman?' Yet even as the words were out, she was remembering that it made a difference to John, all right. And if that letter had told her one thing, it was clearly that he didn't love her. Not enough to remain supportive of her in a demanding job, when, if it had been the other way round, he would have expected it of her as a matter of right.

She was sitting bolt upright in bed, the flowers forgotten for the moment in her lap, her eyes on Philip's face in a steady gaze. She still had the ingenuous look of a child who had suffered a wrong, but who nevertheless was perfectly confident it could be put right again. More than anything, it seemed to Philip, she resembled a small outraged robin. He couldn't help it, he had to turn his head to hide a smile. And there was the dress hanging on Maggie's wardrobe, its shimmering material redolent of nightlife and pleasure and so exactly like the slinky little numbers that had filled his wife's closets, each cut so bare as to leave little to the imagination.

Philip stood up, tight-lipped, telling himself it was no business of his how Maggie spent her life, or with whom. But Nigel? he thought, mistakenly. Then he shrugged. It would be all too easy to let his own keen disappointment in his marriage colour his judgment, when for all he knew Nigel might be the perfect partner for Maggie. With difficulty he dragged his mind back to what had been said.

'To answer your question, Maggie,' he said heavily, 'if the job is important to the person holding it, man or woman, then there really is no difference. It's only later, you see, when there are children . . .' His eyes lingered on her face and there was a terrible sadness in them, Maggie thought, and then walking to the door he turned, a faint smile on his lips. 'Look after yourself now.' And then there was just his footsteps on the stairs.

Maggie sat for a long time, left with the beautiful sunshiny daffodils and the awful totality of her decision. There was a fearful, paralysing longing to weep. And she wept now, because at last she knew without a doubt that John wasn't the right man for her, had known it for a long time. She had confused deep affection for love. But however fond she was of him, it wasn't enough to base a marriage on, and John knew it in his heart, as well as she. He just had not faced up to the fact yet. Even so, Maggie wasn't ready for the pain she felt, as slowly she took the ring from her finger, for she was going to lose a man whom she had known and trusted for a long time, and it hurt—it hurt terribly. Nor could she tell how much of her confusion was due to Philip. Without question, he had aroused certain powerful feelings in her. Feelings that were not reciprocated—oh, he had made that painfully clear. She meant nothing to him, obviously, nothing at all. But tomorrow she would have to talk to John, tell him everything . . . well, practically everything. And then she would make use of some of that accumulated leave, and go home for a few days.

The next morning John sat on the sofa opposite her, already a stranger. Maggie had wondered hopelessly how to start, but then John had taken the initiative, and despite the inevitable pain they had discussed their problems honestly and fully for over an hour, both finally agreeing it best to call their engagement off and make a complete break of it. And so it was over.

'Why don't you let me take you to the train?' John asked, as they waited in the hallway for the cab to come and pick her up.

Maggie hesitated. 'No,' she said at last, her voice low. 'Thanks, John, but it's best if I just go. And anyway, you have to get back to work.'

John shrugged and moved restlessly, his hands stuck into his jacket pockets. He stubbed the toe of his shoe against the skirting-board several times before saying anything, head lowered. Maggie looked wan and exhausted, and he had been more than willing to see the episode as an unfortunate but entirely forgivable lapse on Maggie's part—a bout of nerves in a bride-to-be overwrought by stress and lack of sleep. And yet he knew they were doing the only sensible thing in breaking up. Only, left to him, John brooded, he might not have found the courage to end it, for Maggie was very dear to him. 'That damned job,' he muttered, venting his spleen as always on the hospital. 'I'd like to get my hands on your precious surgeon! It's not the Dark Ages any longer where you nurses are expected to work all hours . . .'

But already there was an air of resignation about his face, and Maggie was quick to notice. She heard the cab outside and stood up, and John bent down and picked up her case. It was time to go.

'Regards to your dad, Maggie.' He kissed her on the cheek. She hesitated. If he had taken her into his arms then, even then, and kissed her, really kissed her . . . A flush swept her face as her thoughts went to Philip.

Then he was handing her into the back seat, and as he stood back waving she was suddenly blinded by tears. He looked so dear and familiar, so very safe somehow. When they were around the corner and out of sight, she covered her face with a trembling hand. She felt so horribly alone all of a sudden. They had been a couple, relied on each other, cared, and had been content to shut off the rest of the world and shelter in their relationship, and now she was on her own again.

CHAPTER FOUR

DETECTIVE-INSPECTOR Hadley Bell was waiting on the platform as the train pulled into York station, a tall lean man whose diffident manner belied a pair of sharp intelligent eyes that observed and recorded everything. Maggie had lost weight, her face small and white against her flaming mass of red hair, but she still carried her head with undeniable spirit, chin at the old defiant angle, and as he reached out his arms, she ran into them.

'Bonny lass!' He held her out at arm's length, gazing at her, then kissed her soundly on both cheeks. 'Looks to me you could do with some good Yorkshire cooking,' he commented when at last he released her.

'Oh, Dad!' And then a wet nose and long slobbering tongue demanded her full attention and she bent to hug Rufus, their shaggy Alsatian dog.

Brownie was on the front steps as the car pulled up. Although her name was Molly Mackay, she had been called Brownie as long as Maggie could remember, after the delicious prize-winning chocolate and walnut squares she baked. After affectionately greeting her, Maggie lingered before going in. The old stone house had taken on an unusually smart appearance, with fresh paint on the doors and windowsills, and the garden too was freshly dug over, the lawns trimmed and the roses pruned; apart from pulling the odd weed, Maggie's father was inclined to leave the plants to look after themselves. Consequently the front of the house had always looked like a wilderness. Slightly puzzled by this new neat appearance, Maggie went on into the house, which was Brownie's domain and was always neat and smelt of lemon verbena furniture polish.

It was harder, much harder than she had expected. When Brownie had gone to her sister's for the evening and Maggie was sitting down to an early supper, her father asked, 'How's John? I thought he would have driven you up.'

Suddenly the carefully rehearsed words stuck in her throat and she didn't know what to say. John was one of them, Yorkshire born and bred. Her father thought of him as a son. Maggie moistened her lips. 'Dad . . .' she began.

'Be up to take you back, is that it?' he asked with a chuckle as he carved off a slice from the pink slab of beef. Glancing up, he paused before placing it on her plate. 'Think you can manage? You said something about a tummy upset.'

'Oh, I'm on the mend now. Dad . . .'

'Good,' he interrupted, carving another slice, 'because we can't have you looking sick for your wedding. Last time I talked to John he was keen to have it soon, and I agreed. The sooner the better. Then once he gets his transfer, you'll both be able to live up here.'

'Dad,' Maggie blurted out in desperation, 'we're not getting married. I broke it off.'

He had noticed the change in her, but had accepted it as Maggie had told him on the phone that she had been ill with some kind of virus. Her face had always been rounded; now it was thinner, pointed, all eyes, her milky skin more translucent than ever. Hadley couldn't bear to see her unhappy. Reaching out a hand, he laid it over hers. 'All right, lass, let's have it, then.'

It was a relief to talk, and just like in the old days, Maggie talked as they ate their meal because she had learned long ago that this might be the only time she would see him, for rarely if ever did her father have a free evening. Of Philip she said not a word. There seemed little point in bringing up his name when her father would never meet him.

'I don't know,' she said with a shake of her curly head, 'I felt I was hiding behind a comfortable relationship, as if—as if I was using John as some kind of fail-safe device.' She flushed, her eyes shifting anxiously to his face. 'Can you understand, am I making any sense?'

He smiled and nodded, and she pushed aside her

food, half eaten. 'Sometimes I wonder if anything does any more,' she admitted wearily. With quiet despair she added, 'I've made a mess of everything, haven't I?'

'No,' he said slowly, 'it doesn't seem that way to me. You came to a decision, and who can tell whether it will be the best one for you? The main thing is, you made it for the best reasons, and leaving a safe relationship isn't the easiest thing in the world. Neither is your job, by the sound of it.' He paused, frowning. 'I don't know, Maggie, maybe you're trying to take too much on at once. Experience is a great thing, and if this woman has as much as you say, then it stands to reason she'll be the best candidate for the position. Now the hard thing,' he added, giving her a shrewd glance, 'is admitting the need for it and going back to taking orders. That's the tough one, by Jove!'

Later on in bed Maggie heard the phone ring, and as so often in the past, she sat up hugging her knees to listen for the crunch of gravel as he drove the car away. He never let up, her father. Maggie's mother had died, the victim of a stupid, senseless crime—it had unleashed a single-minded determination in Hadley Bell that had taken him to the top and had made him into one of the hardest working, most respected police officers in the country. As Maggie pondered, the door pushed open and Rufus padded in to stand with his muzzle pressed on her bed, looking up at her with pleading eyes.

She took his grizzled head in her hands, laughing a little. 'All right then,' she said softly, 'jump up.' The sight of him curled in blissful content at the foot of her bed made her feel happy again.

I'll come home, she thought. Her father would never marry again now; she should be here. It wouldn't be difficult finding a job at the local hospital, and what a relief to get away from London and start again, away from the things that had happened and which had only made her confused and unhappy. Carefully she settled everything in her mind. She would not tell a soul, but in April she would hand in her notice and then finish at the hospital when her holidays began in May.

Now that her mind was made up, Maggie's strength and health began to return and she settled down to enjoy the rest of her stay. Brownie was just as convinced Maggie's recovery was due to her excellent cooking, and when the time came she packed a tin full of her chocolate walnut squares for Maggie to take back with her to London. She also had plenty of advice.

'No skipping meals because you can't find the time, or any such nonsense! Coming home all skin and bone . . .' Maggie grinned at the gross exaggeration and let Brownie have her say. 'Now you take this lass down the street . . . Spends a fortune at the supermarket, and I've seen what's in her cart—rubbish—nothing but rubbish! Couldn't sustain a rat. Now when you get back to London . . .'

Maggie looked about her one last time. She wasn't looking forward to going back, but she thought—hugging her secret to herself—it wouldn't be for long.

Her father drove her to the station. Maggie sat in her peaceful, dreamy isolation by his side. She seemed happier, but there was something wrong somewhere, he could feel it, and he was saddened, because she had never kept anything from him before.

'Got your tin of brownies?' he asked, as Maggie was about to step up into the carriage. 'If there's anything . . . anything you might be worried about, let me know,' he pleaded, and she smiled and nodded. 'Of course, now don't you worry.' Hadley sighed, and had to be content with that.

London lay under a late fall of soiled snow, and Maggie stared gloomily out a grimy window as the bus crawled through the evening rush-hour traffic. They passed the hospital, and it looked even more of a crazy jumble of buildings to Maggie. She wondered how Beth Liddell was.

Letting herself into the house, she dumped her case and made for the kitchen and a hot pot of tea. It was early evening and no one was home yet. She opened the tin and looked at the tempting array of chocolate squares; there was nothing that could compare with home cooking, and once again her thoughts turned to Beth. One of the nurses had said there never seemed to be any visitors from home for Beth, ever.

Feeling pleased and much happier, and carrying a small festively wrapped box, Maggie stopped by the hospital reception desk. 'Sister Bell, what you done to yourself, girl?' Maggie wiped a finger down her nose, suspecting a smut. 'You got colour in your cheeks!'

'Oh!' She burst out laughing, delighted. 'Is that all? For a moment I wondered . . . Tell me, please, which ward is Beth Liddell in now?' She waited a moment before being told Beth was still in Intensive Care. It was an ominous sign: Maggie had hoped Beth would have been transferred to the relatively cheerful wards by now.

The hospital was deceptively quiet—it was the tea hour and few people were about, the day staff having departed and the evening visitors not yet in evidence. All was quiet and calm in the corridor leading to the theatres too, but Maggie quickened her step, just to be on the safe side; she didn't want to go bumping into Philip Lonsdale. Damn it, she thought, as her heart gave a painful bump, he was the very last person she wanted to see!

The curtains around Beth's cubicle were fully drawn. Maggie waited outside for the nurse to be finished with whatever procedure she was doing—and then heard Philip's unmistakable voice. She tried to ignore it—she had to meet him some time. It was ridiculous, there was nothing between them. It was about time she forgot what had happened.

All the same, it would be better to go, and come back later. But even as she was turning away, a nurse hurrying out with a hypodermic tray recognised her, smiled a greeting and called back over her shoulder, 'Oh, Beth, you have a visitor, Sister Bell is here to see you.'

'Oh no, not if you're busy—I'll come back later,' Maggie whispered, and thrust the box into the nurse's hands. 'If you could give this to Beth.'

'Why not give it to her yourself?' asked Philip drily, appearing at the gap in the curtains.

Maggie stared desperately at the box, now returned to her hands, then she lifted her head and smiled. 'Why not?' Philip stood casually aside, one dark brow slightly raised, his shirt collar unbuttoned at the neck, the slimly knotted tie loosened. She thought she had forgotten how handsome he was.

Beth's arm was still in a high sling, she was very pale, and the winged brows were in a tight worried line—in startling contrast to the high serene forehead—but her smile was welcoming as she recognised Maggie. After a little explanation, Maggie handed her the box, and it was only when Beth was plucking at the string that an awful thought struck her. She glanced up at Philip. 'I hope Beth isn't on a restricted intake?' and he raised an amused brow. 'Now you're asking?' They both looked at Beth as she cried, 'Brownies! Oh, I do love them—thank you!' Her face was more vivacious than Maggie had ever seen it, and she felt a surge of pleasure.

'Would you mind, Beth, if I showed Sister Bell how your leg is coming along?' He glanced at Maggie with a pleased smile. 'You can see for yourself how well her arm is doing. Curl your fingers around mine, Beth —good girl! See, a full range of movement.' He folded back the covers from the foot of the bed and removed the protective shield, explaining as he did the treatment Beth was on and running his fingers proudly over five warm toes. The leg was still bandaged to the knee; he explained how the wound looked and asked Beth to tell Maggie how it felt.

Beth nodded and co-operated cheerfully, then the nurse came in to say there was a young man to see her. 'Oh, it's Harry!' Beth said excitedly. 'Please could we have some tea—for the brownies Sister Bell brought me?' Her face was eager and alight, and Philip exchanged a wink with Maggie.

'We must be off, then,' he told Beth. 'Remember to wiggle those toes every so often.' With a broad smile he propelled Maggie out ahead of him.

'I wasn't planning to stay on and play gooseberry,'

Maggie told him, slightly nettled, in the empty corridor outside the unit.

He smiled indulgently at her. 'My word, a trip home has done you good! Maybe you should figure on keeping more regular hours now you're back.'

'You sound just like my father,' Maggie said tartly, pleased she could answer him coolly, when she didn't feel cool at all. He grinned, studying the new boyish haircut. 'I like the hairdo too—now then,' he glanced at his watch, 'I've got half an hour, why don't we go and see young James? Remember that little tyke with the cut fingers?' Maggie hesitated but a moment, then fell into step with him as he moved off easily.

James, in an enormous pair of striped hospital pyjamas, was sitting up in bed dolefully chanting. 'I wanna drink o' water, I wanna drink . . .' His eyes lit up in expectation when he saw the tall dark man come down the ward. 'Mr Lonsdale, Mr Lonsdale . . . I wanna drink o' water!' He came bounding to his feet, jumping up and down on the bed.

Philip caught him in his arms. 'I think we might be able to arrange something—now, young man, this is the lady I was telling you about.'

A pair of angelic eyes surveyed Maggie. 'Is she the one what helped you operate on my fingers?' James asked solemnly. 'She's pretty,' he added with a sigh.

Philip agreed with a smile. 'Now show her what you can do.' James held up his fingers, perfectly straight, then he curled them up with a gleeful chuckle. 'See, they don't hurt any more, do they?' Philip glanced at Maggie. 'The sutures came out day before yesterday. Home tomorrow—right, James?'

'Yep. I wanna drink . . . Nurse says I'll spill it all over my blankets like last time, but I wouldn't, I promise,' he pouted, and Philip laughed.

'A little drink, and we won't tell Nurse, but you must be careful not to spill it.'

It was obvious Philip Lonsdale loved children, and that they loved him. Watching, Maggie thought back to the evening she'd had to say late because of James's fingers, and she remembered John's surliness and sighed; it wasn't fair to compare John with Philip, because unless you worked in a hospital, it was difficult to understand—and what did it matter now anyway?

With James at last settled happily, Maggie asked, as they walked back along the corridor, 'How old is your son?'

Philip glanced down. 'Tim? He'll be eight next month. He started at my old school last September.' He paused, frowning. 'His letters are nothing to go by, but the last time I saw him, which was only a few weeks back, he seemed well enough.'

Unthinking, Maggie asked as she hurried to keep up with his long stride, 'He's at boarding school, then?'

'Anything wrong with boarding schools?' he asked, and Maggie, glancing up, felt the dart of those blue eyes.

'Well,' she faltered, 'it's not what I would choose for my son.'

Philip's mouth twisted. 'Indeed?' he said, in such a way Maggie felt her cheeks begin to burn. She had forgotten the circumstances of his life, and she felt like kicking herself. Of course he would have to send his son to boarding school. His ex-wife, so she understood, spent her time in the world's holiday resorts sunning herself.

'Had anything to eat yet?' Philip paused before pushing open the next set of fire doors waiting for her answer, and Maggie, startled by the sheer abruptness of the question, shook her head slowly. 'Have dinner with me, then,' he said, rather curtly, wondering why he had made the offer when all he wanted was a quick bite and an evening's relaxation watching the box.

'Thank you all the same,' Maggie managed to say in a passably steady voice, despite her heart thumping so loudly she thought he must surely be aware of it, 'but I think I ought to be getting home.'

Instead of relief, which her polite refusal should have produced, Philip felt a surge of annoyance. 'Why?' he demanded. 'Have you something better to do?' And he thought that if she looked at him any longer with those large grey eyes he was going to make a fool of himself and end up having to beg her. Before he allowed such an appalling thing to happen he took her gently by the crook of her arm and said, 'Come along, we'll go over the road, it's a quiet little restaurant and they know me there.' And when she gave a grave little nod, he felt like picking her up and hugging her. Dear God! he thought.

When they had been divested of their coats and Maggie was studying the menu, he studied her. She looked very demure in her white cotton blouse with its frilled upturned collar and Black Watch tartan wool shift that skimmed her figure and fell in box-pleats to midcalf. Indigo ribbed wool stockings and black pumps completed the outfit. It was what her mother had insisted she wear, he was certain, and he said with a faint smile, 'I like what you're wearing. Much more you.'

Maggie stared at him over the top of her menu. What did he mean? She had on the kind of thing she always wore. 'I'm glad you like it,' she said in a somewhat guarded voice, 'but why is it much more me?'

He raised his eyebrows and said drily, 'The last time I saw you, there was this shimmery thing, and you had on a flesh pink Mae West affair.'

Maggie couldn't think what the shimmery thing was that he referred to, having forgotten about Liv's dress. 'Oh, Philip . . .' she said, and paused, her cheeks flaming, for it was the first time she had called him anything other than sir, or Mr Lonsdale. Recovering quickly, she said, 'That was just something I picked up for a song at the market. You know, it's very old, and it's crêpe-de-Chine, which is much more comfortable to wear than nylon.'

Looking at the shy embarrassed face in front of him, Philip wondered if he could have been wrong in thinking she led some kind of double life. Wearing large baggy hospital gowns by day, responsible, conscientious, running an efficient theatre—and at night? Did she really go out in dresses like the one he had seen hanging on her wardrobe door? He moved restlessly in his chair; there had been no doubt she had looked damned sexy in that pink thing in bed—the memory still bothered him. He dragged his eyes from her face and pretended to be searching for the wine waiter. 'The food might be good,' he grumbled, 'but they're damned slow with the service.'

When they had been served with an excellent meal of steak and jacket potatoes and salad, and Philip had filled her glass with a dry red wine, Maggie asked, 'Why is Beth still in the unit?'

He glanced at her. 'I want to keep her under my eye. Her prognosis depends on our being able to deal swiftly with any arterial occlusion that develops. At the moment she's still on anti-coagulants, so that minimises the danger of a thrombus, but we can't overlook the possibility of one forming when we take her off.'

'Is that likely, another thrombus might form?' Maggie asked, and he smiled coldly.

'Anything is likely.' He sat in silence, his eyes intent on the wine glass in front of him. Maggie stared at his profile—the broad high forehead, the curve of his brows, the determined jaw—what was he thinking, what was he weighing up? He lifted his head and found her watching him. 'Ah, Maggie,' he confessed, 'she worries me. Beth's arm is fine, you saw the range of movement yourself, and her leg? Well, to be honest, it's dicey. But that in itself isn't the worrying factor, it has something to do with her, something I can't quite put my finger on.'

Maggie sat very still. She was thinking about the second time Beth came to Theatre. As if to herself, she said, 'Her hold on life is tenuous.' She lifted her eyes to him. 'Remember, I tried to tell you once—I said I thought she could slip away from us.'

'Yes, you did,' he said softly, his eyes dark, dark blue. Maggie felt herself going soft inside, as for a long time he said nothing, but sat looking at her, then his mouth curved into a wry smile. 'And you were right and I think I knew it, though at the time, I remember, I couldn't let myself think about it or I'd never have gone through with the operation.'

'But you did, and it was a success,' she reminded him, and he nodded slowly.

'Let's just hope it's a lasting one,' he said, in an odd voice, then collecting himself, he leaned forward and a smile broke his seriousness. 'Now, Sister Bell, when are you coming back to us?'

The words were in themselves pleasing—but it was the warmth with which they had been spoken that caused a flush of happiness in Maggie. Already she was looking forward to being back at work, her mind absorbing his smallest gestures, even the slight inflection of his brow before he reached out his hand . . . Somewhat distracted by her train of thought, Maggied turned her attention to answering his question.

'Tomorrow,' she told him with a smile. 'I left a note on Paula's desk to say, and knowing Paula, I'm sure she can fit me in somewhere.' She took a sip of wine and lowered the glass, her face impassive, because he was watching her like a hawk and she couldn't let him know the effort it cost to say what she had to. 'I haven't applied for Fiona's position,' Maggie said quietly. 'I thought about it, then decided that perhaps I could use some more experience before taking on such a job. I expect, though, that Claudia will make an excellent Theatre Sister.' Philip was grinning from ear to ear, and she thought crossly, he's pleased as Punch, Claudia has the job in the palm of her little hand.

But in fact, Philip was enjoying an enormous sense of relief. He had been worried that Maggie might get herself involved in a power struggle with Claudia, or worse, throw in the towel altogether. But he had underestimated her—here she was, no fuss, no recriminations, quietly prepared to go on and do her job; he himself was delighted Claudia had arrived to take on the burden of running the show, leaving Maggie where he needed her most. Let Claudia do the hatchet work, just so long as it meant Maggie was free to assist him; there wasn't another nurse to touch her in that department. He thought with pleasure that she would be there tomorrow, on the other side of the operating table, quietly confident in what she was doing; he let out a sigh and started to relax, forgetting for the moment the other imagined side to her that made him so angry.

Not noticing her withdrawal, he made easy conversation, joking lightheartedly, while Maggie did a slow burn. She was thinking that he might at least have had the grace to conceal his obvious delight in her stepping down; what a Theatre Sister she must have made, she thought gloomily, if the surgeon had to bring in another candidate for the job!

'What happened?' Philip had only then discovered Maggie wasn't wearing her engagement ring, and he looked up with the startled enquiry. 'Or doesn't the ring go with today's clothes?' he added snidely.

Perhaps he had meant it as a joke, but Maggie was no longer in the mood to take it—and the rotten insinuation. 'Oh, as a matter of fact, I'm having the diamonds changed to rubies,' she said, adding facetiously, 'So much more me, don't you think?'

The little minx, Philip thought, and scowled. That butter-wouldn't-melt-in-her-mouth look of hers; he should have done a lot more than just kiss her the other day when she fell into his arms. Had she done it deliberately? Philip pondered.

'Excuse me, sir.' Philip, startled, looked up as the head waiter murmured his message. 'Hospital operator on the phone for you.' He nodded. Maggie's interest seemed taken up exclusively by the pianist: an oily type with bleached hair and flashy bow tie. Well, let her—He got up and went over to the phone.

Why did she have to go and be so thin-skinned? Maggie wondered, miserably aware that she should have treated the remark as a joke, which he probably meant it as. But it was the tone of voice that had set her off. She sighed, and, not yet ready to lose face, feigned an interest in the list of desserts when she saw him coming back.

'You go ahead, order whatever you want, I've told them to put it on my bill. I have to get back.'

When Maggie raised her head, he was already walking away.

CHAPTER FIVE

MAGGIE shifted from one aching foot to the other and wondered how much longer Duncan was going to take. With maddening slowness the Registrar threaded in the last suture, then stepped back, squinting his eyes in concentration. 'Not bad,' he said, and gave the suture line one last little prod. The anaesthetist—not Alan Bradford this morning—glanced up with a frown. The patient would be awake on the table at this rate; in his opinion the knee needed a few stitches, not elaborate embroidery.

There had been the usual Saturday morning casualties. So far, they had restored an ear lobe to its inebriated owner; plucked a large chicken bone from a girl's throat, despite the mother's insistence that her daughter was a strict vegetarian; and now this footballer with his injured knee.

When asked for her opinion, Maggie stopped to inspect Duncan's meticulous handiwork. 'Lovely job,' she murmured, and meant it. Duncan was a good surgeon and his patients stood an excellent chance of regaining full use of an injured part; given they were strong enough to stand a long anaesthetic in the first place. She picked up the surgical spray ready to cover the wound, but Duncan shook his head.

'I know Philip likes that stuff, but personally I think it keeps the infection in, rather than out.' It was an old bone of contention, and Maggie rather favoured keeping the wound sealed argument; however, it was the surgeon's prerogative and she was happy to go along with it.

The anaesthetist thought it was just Duncan flapping his wings and gritted his teeth. 'Can we finish before the man wakes up?'

'Just a gauze dressing and crêpe bandage, Maggie,'

Duncan said calmly, before casually glancing at the patient's face. 'Is he all right? I don't like his colour.' The implication being that short operations were about the level of the anaesthetist's competence. Satisfied his insult had found its mark, he stood aside for Gary to finish up.

As Gary stood holding the leg for Maggie to bandage, his eyes met hers and crinkled at the corners above his mask—they were used to Duncan's sniping and accepted it, more often than not, as part of his temperament. 'Got yourself a half day,' he said, watching her wind the bandage in a figure of eight and wondering how on earth she managed to end up with a perfect V in front. 'Bit of luck getting them off on a Saturday?'

'Think so?' Maggie smiled, her hands busy. She felt she had earned the half day. There had been the four weekdays she had worked since coming back—now the weekend, then she was expected to do a week of late shifts with several nights on call. Yet, when she thought about it, she didn't mind; the busier she was, the less time she had to brood. Claudia had been on opposite duties, and that she hadn't minded either. On Monday, Claudia would officially take charge of the theatre. Maggie accepted it as a fact of life, and those people who had urged her to at least make a late application for the position met with little response. She had listened closely to her father's good advice and was content to abide by it and gain the experience she needed.

It was after midday when the cleaning had been done and the theatre made ready for the next case; Maggie decided not to join Bronwyn and Sue for lunch in the hospital cafeteria, electing instead to go home and see what Jane was up to. She still half expected John to be waiting for her in his car, and then she would remember, with a strange flat absence of emotion, that her life was her own now.

Except for one small boy the waiting area immediately outside the theatre complex was deserted; as Maggie hurried past, all she could see of the child was his curly head bent over a magazine, a pair of grubby knees and grey school socks which had slipped in folds around his black school shoes.

'Excuse me, miss.' Maggie stopped and turned round. The boy was standing up, and his eyes were so large and anxious she felt an instant concern for him. Walking back, she said, 'Hello, whatever's the matter?' And when he still said nothing, she asked, 'Are you waiting for someone?'

His eyes slid at last from her face and fastened on the closed theatre doors with a tinge of desperation. 'My father,' he said.

Maggie asked gently, 'Now who might your father be?'

'Mr Lonsdale, miss.'

Maggie stared at him. 'Why then, you must be Timothy.'

But he shook his head. 'No—I'm called Tim,' he declared.

'Well . . .' Maggie smiled; not many people called her Margaret, either. 'Is he expecting you, Tim?' she asked solemnly, and he hunched his shoulders, pouting.

'Not exactly.'

Maggie lowered her eyes. Tim was rather too like his father for comfort—apart from a purely professional capacity, she had seen little of Philip these past days, and after her facetious remarks the other night at dinner, she didn't imagine she would see very much more of him either. This morning he had been in to do his rounds, she knew that at least, but where he was at the moment she had no idea.

'I'll go and ring round for him, shall I?' she said, smiling down at the boy's upturned face. 'You stay here, I won't be long.'

It took her only five minutes to find out that Philip had left the hospital, but had not as yet returned to his home. 'You could get him on his bleeper,' Tim said, when she had told him.

Maggie shook her head. 'He isn't on call this weekend, so he won't have it with him, but I do know he'll be checking in every so often, because he has a patient he's very worried about.' As Tim's face fell, she asked, 'Had any lunch yet?' and he shook his head. 'Well, why don't you come home and have some with me? I'll leave a message on your father's answer-phone. How about it?'

The effect was miraculous, and Tim's enthusiasm outweighed any doubts Maggie might have had about the wisdom of such an invitation; Philip might have some kind of aversion to the household she lived in, but he could hardly object to her rescuing his son. Over a lunch of fried eggs, sausages, tomatoes, chips and oodles of hot buttered toast, the story came out at last. Tim confessed to having run away from school; he had spent every last penny on a train fare to London.

'Oh dear,' murmured Maggie, but remembering only too well the strange terrors that had beset her own early schooldays—and she had been able to return to the friendly warmth of Brownie's kitchen each afternoon. Tim's eyes had again grown large and worried, and she reached out a hand to smooth back a lock from his brow. How thick and springy his hair was, she thought, how very much like Philip's.

'Here now,' she said, 'finish your lunch first before you start worrying. Afterwards, we'll think what to do for the best.' She thought how like Brownie she sounded, and also that she had unwittingly involved herself in Tim's escapade.

Reassured, Tim happily demolished the rest of his lunch. 'Do you live here by yourself?' he mumbled, looking around the kitchen, his mouth full.

'You'd think so, wouldn't you?' Maggie said with a smile. 'In fact, I only pay rent and share the house. The owner is out—and so is Jane.' She explained who Jane was, and at the same time it flashed through her mind that Jane was conspicuous by her absence these days. But there was little time to puzzle over the mystery. As they were stacking the dirty dishes, the front door crashed open and the accompanying shouts and hoots of laughter advertised Nigel's return.

'Is that the owner?' Tim asked.

'I told you he was noisy.' But even Maggie was unprepared for what happened next—when a pair of horns and gleaming eyes appeared round the doorpost, and was followed clumsily by the body of a large black and white cow. Tim jumped up and down in excitement; as far as he was concerned, Maggie's housemates were fun.

Nigel appeared with a large box in his arms. 'Shoo!' he said to the cow, as if he was used to finding one in his kitchen when he came home. 'Hello, who have we here?' he asked when he saw Tim.

'Tim Lonsdale,' said Maggie, choking with laughter at the strange hairy animal, who was by now collapsing in a heap.

'This is Liv,' Nigel added, introducing the attractive girl who had walked in, her arms laden with curious items. He went on to explain about the charity ball they were dressing up for that evening. Maggie remembered having seen the notices up on the hospital information boards, and although given the grand title of Charity Ball, really it was an evening of fun for families who were being encouraged to dress up as characters in Alice in Wonderland. Proceeds were to go to a day care centre for cerebral palsy handicapped children.

Tim was admiring the cow costume, and when invited, climbed eagerly into the hindquarters. Then he tried out the Rabbit costume Liv produced, and begged Nigel to dress up as well.

'Maggie, you and Tim had better come along tonight,' Nigel said goodhumouredly.

Maggie frowned and bit her lip. 'I think maybe Tim's father will want him home tonight,' she said, then added quickly, seeing the boy's disappointment, 'But we could ask.'

'I've never been to a real ball,' sighed Tim.

'Oh, it's not really a ball—more like a Mad Hatter tea party,' said Liv. 'Here, I'll help you get into this. Oh look, you'd make a much better White Rabbit than me. You can wear it if you like—I'd much rather go as Alice anyway.'

She looked very like an Alice, Maggie thought, with her small delicate features and long flaxen hair. Liv was nice, much nicer than the girls Nigel usually ran around with.

When Nigel came in they fell about in screams of laughter, for he made a perfect Duchess. 'Baby,' said Nigel, looking around, 'I must have a baby.' He snatched up a tea towel and fashioned it around the oven cloth, then cradled it in both arms. When the front door bell rang he gave a wicked grin and went off to answer it, the rest crowding behind to watch the fun.

In the excitement, Maggie had quite forgotten Philip, and she was still laughing when Nigel threw open the door; it took her a moment to realise he was there, standing rather grimly on their front step. His composure was admirable, she had to give him that. He looked with apparent concern at the bundle in Nigel's arms. 'Madam,' he intoned, 'your child appears to be sickening for something.'

As if nothing in this curious household could possibly surprise him, Philip's eyes passed from one to the other, dismissed the White Rabbit as incidental, and finally came to rest sardonically on Maggie. 'There's a somewhat garbled message on my answer-phone,' he said, pleasantly enough. 'Perhaps you can explain?'

Maggie swallowed, and glanced nervously at Tim's bobbing ears as the boy jiggled up and down in his costume, impatiently waiting for his father to recognise him—though there was little chance of that as even his face was covered with stuck-on whiskers. Sensing a drama, Liv grabbed Nigel by the arm. 'Duchess, it's time we disappeared.'

Struggling to sound perfectly normal, Maggie invited Philip inside, and he stepped into the hallway. 'All right, but only for a moment. What's all this about Tim?'

'Dad, it's me!' shouted Tim, unable to contain himself any longer. Philip's eyes swept over the White Rabbit in real shock. Tim unzipped his furry chin and pulled back the head, while Maggie, watching unhappily, clasped and unclasped her hands. It was enough, she suspected, arriving to find a runaway son . . . But as a White Rabbit in a bizarre cast of characters?

Philip's startled look had turned to deep concern. It was not so much the costume—there must be some logical explanation forthcoming—but that his son, who he had thought was safely at school, was now in London and to all intents and purposes seemed to be involved with Maggie's scatterbrained friends. That Maggie was somehow responsible for this he didn't doubt for a second. Then as tears welled up in his son's eyes—grey eyes like Maggie's—he quickly sought to bring some normalcy to the situation. The whys and wherefores could be dealt with at a more appropriate time.

'Good lord,' he said gruffly, 'and I thought you were a real rabbit!' He pulled a spanking white handkerchief from his jacket pocket and proceeded to wipe Tim's eyes. 'All right?' he asked gently. When Tim nodded he repocketed the handkerchief and said, 'Better shed your fur and hop down to the car—I'll take you home.'

'I'll just go and give the costume back to Liv,' said Tim, looking up at Maggie with disappointment written all over his face. Maggie nodded, aware of Philip's eyes on her and knowing that anything she could say would be bound to be wrong in his view.

'He was so unhappy . . .' she mumbled, as Tim ran off, not daring to look up, and then Tim was back again, bubbling over with excitement.

'They've got spare tickets for the Ball. Oh, please, please, Dad, can we go? I can wear the Rabbit costume, and you could dress up too!' He stopped for breath, adding hopefully, 'Maggie's going.'

Little did Tim know, Maggie thought despairingly, that he had just given the idea the kiss of death.

Philip raised a cynical brow. 'A ball?' His voice was heavy with sarcasm.

'A Charity Ball . . .' and as the other brow shot up in disbelief, Maggie added hastily, 'Not a regular society ball, no, no,' she managed a little laugh at the very idea of Tim being asked to join in an evening of adult entertainment, then tried her best to explain, with Tim looking on hopefully from one to the other. Maggie felt she was failing him miserably.

When she finished, Tim added hopefully, 'It's for a very good cause.'

'So Miss Bell has explained. However,' Philip put a finger under his son's chin, 'you didn't leave your school to come all this way back to London in order to dress up as a rabbit, whatever the cause. I rather think we'll want a quiet evening—you have some explaining to do. Now, run on down to the car and say hello to Miss Fanslow. You remember her, don't you . . . the lady who went to live in America?'

Claudia was waiting in the car? Maggie stared up at him and Philip was forced to give his son an encouraging pat on the shoulder, 'Come on now,' and Tim nodded, though less than enthusiastic, he turned to Maggie.

'Thank you very much for lunch, it was great,' and then obediently he trudged down the steps. Maggie's heart went out to him.

As soon as he was out of earshot, Philip turned on Maggie, whose eyes were fixed demurely downwards. Inside he was seething. 'That youngster has enough wild schemes of his own, without you involving him in any of yours!' he snapped.

Maggie bristled. 'It's not a wild scheme!'

'Inviting a child of seven to a ball?' His voice was scathing, and Maggie's lips trembled, for she saw she had made it worse for Tim by bringing him to the house, and was bitterly sorry.

'It's not a real ball—I explained that. It's only a grand title for a family evening, there are notices up all round the hospital.' She was looking at him oddly, then suddenly she turned her head away; she was sick and tired of his snide comments—about her friends, and what she did, or what he thought she did, in her free time. What was more, the evening hadn't even been her idea, it had evolved from the others, who knew nothing of the circumstances—was she supposed to have told the world his son had run away from school? For the first time she came very close of hating him. Coldly she said, 'If you didn't have your head stuck in the ground like . . . like an ostrich half the time, you'd have seen them around the hospital for yourself.'

Startled, Philip laughed. But it was a hard unpleasant laugh. 'And I suppose, in your opinion, a child should be rewarded for running away from school?'

'No, of course I don't,' Maggie said furiously. Trust him to twist things! She bit her lip. She couldn't let Tim down, she had to *try*, and say something that would soften his mood. She twisted her hands. 'Perhaps, though, do you think, a little fun wouldn't hurt . . .'

'*Fun?*' His look was blistering. 'You and those Wonderland characters you live with—having fun is all the lot you can think of!'

For a moment she stood staring at him, her eyes filling with tears of rage and humiliation, then she whirled and ran. Philip sprang after her, his footsteps pounding on the stairs behind her. He caught her by the arm and spun her round.

'Damn it, Maggie . . .' he began.

Oh no, she had had enough. 'How dare you be so patronising!' she blazed down at him, tugging at her arm, one foot on the next step prepared for flight the instant she was free. She was panting, the out-thrust of her young breasts rising and falling with her breathing. 'Let my arm go or I'll scream!'

'Go right ahead,' Philip growled at her, 'and I'll give you something to scream about!' She had made him so angry he could scarcely think. All he wanted to do was pull her down to him and kiss her, hard. Something of his intention showed in his expression, and she pulled away from him. Only then did Philip realise the extent of what was happening to him—he fought for control as a passionate longing flooded him to sweep her into his arms and carry her up the stairs and kiss her and keep on kissing her, the feel and look and smell of her . . . Maggie threatened every rational thought he had ever had. He drew back. What she did out of hospital hours had nothing, absolutely nothing to do with him, and he had no right to criticise her, or for that matter, her friends, or the way she lived. No right, he told himself again. Then he realised he was still holding her wrist and he saw the angry red weal beneath his fingers. Immediately he loosened his grip and looked up at her.

'I'm sorry,' he muttered, his voice thick, totally unlike his own. 'Please forget what I said. I didn't mean it.'

Philip Lonsdale never, ever, said a word he did not mean, and this Maggie knew. 'That's not at all like you,' she told him; her voice was angry, but she looked at him, briefly uncertain. 'All I did was give the poor child lunch. And if Nigel and the others tried to cheer him up, what's the harm?'

Grim-faced, his brow furrowed, he said, 'Yes . . . Well, thanks for giving him lunch. But I'd have appreciated it more if you'd left it at that.' The wrist was snatched from his hand, she had wheeled and was running up the stairs as he watched. Philip's hand gripped the banister as he bowed his head over it. Dear God, what was happening to him? His mind was in chaos.

As he heard her bedroom door close with a decisive click, he straightened slowly and turned round; his body as he walked back down felt as heavy as lead. Catching sight of the discarded costumes in the hall, he stalked around them and out the front door, banging it closed. His jaw was clenched tight. Alice in Wonderland, indeed! Well, he could always count on Claudia to be cool, rational, and devastatingly practical; a pity Tim didn't like her more than he did.

From the upstairs window Maggie watched him walk to his car. She was trembling in every limb. She hated the man, and she fiercely denied every other thought to the contrary. If anybody then had suggested she had fallen in love with him, she would have attacked the idea as ludicrous and denied it vehemently.

There had been talk, of course; it would not be a hospital if there wasn't. Maggie had heard about Claudia Fanslow's affair with a married man; it was supposed she had gone to the States to wait until his divorce came through. No one suggested that that man had been

Philip, but it was obvious now to Maggie. She had known it as soon as he told Tim to go out and say hello to Claudia.

But poor Tim? Maggie didn't think Claudia was the type to want a small boy around, especially one who had been as naughty as Tim had. She rested her forehead on the pane of glass, relishing for a moment the delicious coolness against her hot face; she had promised to help, and she had a sad guilty feeling that as far as Tim's father was concerned, she had done anything but. Then the phone rang and Nigel was calling for her up the stairs, and Maggie, going down to answer it, was surprised to hear her father's voice on the line.

Half an hour later Jane came humming up stairs to find Maggie getting ready to go out. 'Mmm,' she commented, stopping to put her head round the door, 'must be someone special!'

'It is,' said Maggie, turning with a smile. 'My father is in London . . . Hi, I like your hair, what have you had done?'

'Cut short the way you said, light perm, streaks . . . ta-da!' Jane preened herself in front of Maggie's admiring eyes, then left again, humming. What was that tune? Maggie wondered. She turned back to the mirror puzzling over it, but the words wouldn't come.

'Married?' A disbelieving look in her eyes, Maggie stared at her father over the pink linen tablecloth in the smart little restaurant he had brought her to. Suddenly she remembered the fresh paint on the house, the trim lawns; she had thought it odd at the time, but it made sense now, of course. Home, she thought, and swallowed a lump in her throat. It would never be the same. It would change, everything would change . . . Her father—it was difficult to imagine him married, another woman in the house, a stranger. And what of her own plans? They would have to be abandoned now.

Then she realised, with a sense of shock, how selfish her first thoughts had been—and not one for his own happiness. She was still looking at him, but this time really seeing him: a prominent aquiline nose on a face still handsome, lean and youthful, and her eyes filled with shame—after all these years he deserved to find someone special. 'Tell me everything,' she said, smiling. 'I want to know—how you met her, what she's like. And—oh, everything!'

Hadley knew his daughter, he knew the shadows that lurked in the grey eyes. So it was with relief that he watched the doubt fade into interest. He thought back a year, to the court case in Australia where he had first met Moira; the weeks they'd had together before his return to England and the long months of correspondence. Then Moira's phone call to say that she was coming. All this he told Maggie. But when he told Maggie that Moira was thirty-one, he knew from the quickly lowered eyes that it shocked her that he was marrying someone so young.

'She's a right bonny lass, Maggie. A Yorkshire lass.' He looked so anxious she impulsively leaned over and planted a kiss on his forehead.

'Dad, if you love her then I'm sure I shall.' She settled back on her chair and picked up the napkin that had slipped from her knees.

'I thought you might like to come out to Heathrow with me in the morning and meet her yourself,' he suggested gently.

Maggie hesitated, undecided. It was not impossible to swop duties—provided she could find someone at this late stage willing to work a Sunday—but it occurred to her that perhaps it would be better if her father and Moira got reacquainted without the added distraction of a daughter. When she demurred, Hadley didn't object, and it was decided Maggie should meet Moira when next she could get a few days off from the hospital to travel home, and it was left at that.

By eight the next morning the hospital had cleared the usual list of Saturday night accidents and was settling down to await the injuries a typical Sunday threw up. Maggie was in the office doing a routine stocktaking of all the recorded drugs that were kept locked in the safe.

When Claudia walked into the room she barely glanced up.

'Lucky for you I'm not an addict for drugs,' Claudia observed, pausing just inside the door.

Maggie started. 'Oh, good heavens—I thought you were Bronwyn!'

Claudia gave her brief smile. 'Exactly. Shouldn't the door to the office be locked when the DDs are out?'

'That's probably not necessary,' Maggie said with a frown. The doors to the unit were locked as a security precaution, and this Claudia knew. Ostensibly nobody could get in without first giving their name over the intercom. But Claudia was looking positively jubilant, so Maggie guessed someone had forgotten to shut them properly on their way in. It happened often, she had to confess, because it was a system they only used at weekends and people were apt to forget. Then she almost smiled. It was now Claudia's job to sort that little problem out. Maggie was merely one of the workers —and quite happy to take orders again. It was tough at the top, she thought, feeling almost shamelessly amused as she watched her new boss pace restlessly around the room, pausing to look at this and straighten that. At last Claudia remembered to stop frowning and turned to deliver a cool smile.

'Funny, isn't it—I never would have thought you led such an interesting social life. Quite a little household you live in, according to Philip.' She permitted herself a light laugh. 'And we all know what a stick-in-the-mud he is!'

'Do we?' Maggie lowered her eyes, surprised at her defensive reaction when she had every reason to agree with Claudia. 'How's Tim?'

'Oh, no need to worry about that young man, he's perfectly all right. He gets his own way over everything—his father spoils him rotten.' That was news to Maggie. 'However,' Claudia snapped, as if the subject were an anathema to her, 'I didn't come to talk about Tim.' No, I'm sure you didn't, Maggie thought, and suppressed a little smile. Tim had quite spoilt Claudia's weekend, by all accounts.

'In fact,' Claudia folded her elegant body into a chair opposite, 'I thought you and I should have a talk.' Maggie watched her warily; there was something about the other that was reminiscent of a well-fed cat. 'You managed to run the place quite well while Fiona was on sick leave, considering the staffing problems you had to contend with.'

Maggie shrugged. 'They all pulled their weight . . .'

'I'm sure—but you must admit, Sue Manning needs a bomb under her.'

Frowning, Maggie stood up and put the boxes containing the drugs back into the cabinet. She said evenly, 'Sue might be on the slow side, but we all have to learn. Sister Brown on Lilley sent her down to us highly recommended.'

'Sister Brown is no racehorse herself,' Claudia replied acidly. 'How do you find Philip Lonsdale?'

'I—well . . .' Maggie flushed in her surprise at the unexpected question. 'He's a brilliant surgeon, highly dedicated, a man . . . who really only cares for his work,' she ended softly.

'My dear,' Claudia interrupted with a conspiratorial little laugh, 'no man cares only about work, believe me. He's a man—isn't he?' The china blue eyes rested on Maggie reflectively, then dismissed her. There was a certain vulnerability some men might find attractive, but she hardly thought that Philip would. However, she wasn't taking any chances. Claudia leaned forward.

'Talking about work—we need a well qualified Sister to take charge of the late shift. Someone with a proven track record and capable of thinking on her feet.' She paused to let her words sink in, her smile shrewd. 'You're the person I want, Maggie. I could trust you to take on that kind of responsibility and make the right decision in the heat of the moment. Right now,' she leaned back and flapped her hand in disgust, 'they're at sixes and sevens, totally unorganised.'

Claudia's blatant attempt at flattery failed miserably

with Maggie, who dismissed it for the bluff it was. Claudia wanted to get her out of the way. It was an old ploy. Besides, she had seen the roster for the coming weeks and knew very well Claudia had marked her down for a heavy run of late shift work. It was usual for staff to be rotated to cover the late hours so that the burden did not fall too heavily on any one person. They all did their turn, and Claudia knew it. But Maggie merely smiled sweetly.

'Does that mean I have a choice, you'd change the roster if I objected to the duties?'

'Are you objecting?' Claudia too was smiling, but the words had a bite on them. Without giving Maggie a chance to answer, she carried on, 'It will be hard graft, I know, but worth it in the long run. We all have to do it to get to the top . . .' She stiffened in annoyance as the door burst open and Bronwyn's head appeared round it. 'Does no one in this place ever think of knocking?'

Bronwyn looked mildly surprised, 'We've made coffee,' she said, then hastily withdrew.

Claudia's face was livid. 'And that's another thing,' she snapped, 'the appalling bad manners of the girls!' She stood up with a jerk. 'Fiona would turn in her grave!'

'She's not in it yet,' Maggie pointed out, quite reasonably, and Claudia said stiffly, 'Oh, don't be so literal, Maggie, you know what I mean.' A tight irritable expression destroyed the youthful line of her face and made Maggie wonder at the age they had guessed her. Thirty-three—Philip's age—had been the consensus of opinion. Thirty-seven had been a shrewd guess from Gary, the department's self-acknowleged expert on such matters.

Later that evening Maggie complained to Jane, 'What made me so mad was that crack about Fee. As though anybody who leaves the department at a certain age is dead and gone!'

'Mmmm . . .' Jane complacently massaged another blob of cream into her face, and Maggie gave her a sharp look. Anything she said to Jane these days was like so much water off a duck's back. There was something else, too, about her that Maggie couldn't quite put her finger on. Giving up, she flopped back on the bed. 'What do you think about my father wanting to get married? After all these years!'

'I think it's lovely,' Jane said suddenly, with surprising passion. 'And do stop making him sound old. He's not. It really is time he was thinking of marrying again, and I think it's lovely.'

'Yes, you said that before,' said Maggie, a trifle sharply. 'And of course I agree. And I didn't say he was old, it's just that she's so much younger. Why, she's more my age than his!'

'Well, that doesn't matter, does it? Age isn't the most important thing when two people love each other.'

'I think it should be a consideration—a big consideration,' Maggie said hotly, 'whether they love each other or not.'

Jane banged on half a pot of cream as she muttered, 'That's all you know about it!'

Maggie sat bolt upright. 'And what's that supposed to mean?'

Picking up a tissue, Jane began scrubbing her face clean. 'If you'd been in love, I mean really in love, you'd know.' A number of expressions flew across Maggie's face, and Jane waited on tenterhooks for an outburst. It didn't come. Maggie pulled a resigned smile and stood up, shrugging tiredly.

'You're right. How would I know?'

There was no bitterness in her voice, only a painful acknowledgement that her thoughts on the matter were a hopeless muddle, and more than that, the fact that Jane knew it. If she had been thinking straight, she might have stopped to wonder why Jane had got so worked up.

That night, Philip Lonsdale and Tim and Claudia and her father and Jane were all mixed up in a dream which seemed to have an Alice in Wonderland setting; where she was the White Rabbit, scurrying around looking for something, continually hastening to some prearranged appointment and then losing her way, and all the while Philip waited with a disdainful smile on his face.

Although she hadn't set her alarm clock, Maggie woke at the usual time for morning duty, and then couldn't go back to sleep. Giving up, she slipped into a robe and went downstairs to join the others for coffee. A little later she put a fruitless call through to her father, only to find he was at work and that Brownie had spent the weekend with her sister and so had not had the chance to meet Moira yet. Then after she was sure Philip would have left for the hospital, she dialled his home phone number, hoping to speak to Tim. There was no answer, and she slowly put the phone down. She had thought there might be a housekeeper to look after the boy, though it was more than likely he had been packed off back to school. Coming on duty, Maggie found she was rostered for the Gynae theatre, along with Pat and Bronwyn. All three were on call for the night and would sleep in the old house surgeons' quarters. They met up in the office to sign on, then went to look at the list for the afternoon's surgery. Bronwyn goaned aloud when she saw they had eight operations crammed into the one session.

'My giddy aunt!' she exclaimed. 'We'll be dropping by the end of that lot!'

The afternoon proceeded as promised. Alec Blakelock, the Gynae Registrar, was known as much for his fund of dubious stories as for his speed, and the pace Maggie could stand, but the off-colour jokes produced a shudder of annoyance.

'Another one about women's troubles, and I'm going,' she muttered to Pat, as they struggled to lift yet another pair of legs into the lithotomy stirrups.

'And me with you,' mumbled Pat from behind the green drapes. But eventually the last case was pushed out, and then there was the mad rush to get along to the canteen for something to eat before the acutes started coming in.

Two appendicectomies and one herniorrhaphy later Maggie crawled into bed, too tired to sit up in the common room talking. The phone rang by her bed just as she was drifting off to sleep. 'Hello . . . Sister Bell.'

'Sorry to wake you,' it was Philip's voice, 'but we'll have to bring Beth Liddell back to theatre and operate immediately.' Maggie sat up, instantly awake. They had both been dreading this.

Philip was in the office when she arrived to unlock the drug cupboard. With his hair unbrushed and the shadow of a beard on his chin he looked tired, and yet her heart missed a beat at the sight of him.

He glanced up from the notes he was reading. 'This may be a bit complicated, though it's hard to say at this point. Depends if we can remove the thrombus without causing too much damage, but in any case, it usually involves some arterial reconstruction . . .' He spoke quietly, explaining the procedure, confident there would be no recriminations; Maggie could be relied on to operate at a highly professional level and not be obstructive because of some personal animosity. As she turned to go and start the preparations he asked, 'How long are you going to be on afternoons?'

'I'm sorry, I don't really know,' Maggie answered politely.

Philip glared. 'Well, it's ridiculous putting you in the Gynae theatre. Your expertise could be put to more profitable use with us.'

'It's not up to me,' Maggie reminded him dispassionately.

Philip said, rather shortly, 'I'm aware of that. I'll get it arranged—I'm not having you stuck in there every afternoon . . . Now can we make a start?'

'Can I see Beth first?' asked Maggie, her eyes on his face. His expression softened.

'Of course,' he shrugged quickly. 'Make it short, though.' He watched her go. She had the power to move him unbearably. She was spirited, yet could be passive and at the same time enormously strong. She had warmth and compassion, and he wondered if that ass she was going to marry knew it. If? She *was* going to marry. He hadn't seen the ring on her finger.

Maggie found Beth in a highly strung state. Alan, unfortunately, was not on call that night and the young anaesthetist who had taken his place betrayed a nervousness that infected them all, even Bronwyn. Beth was insisting on seeing Philip, and the anaesthetist's brow was wrinkled with impatience; he was just as adamant that she couldn't see him. Eventually Maggie slipped away and went to see the surgeon herself.

'I think all she wants is some reassurance that you won't amputate,' she told him.

Philip looked at her over the top of his mask, then he heaved a sigh and rinsed the soap from his arms. 'I've already explained . . . But I'll come,' he agreed.

Finally they got Beth fully anaesthetised to the table —and with the anaesthetist in a genial mood now that his patient was stable, they were able to proceed. As far as Maggie could tell, the operation went as Philip had anticipated. He was able to successfully remove the thrombus and restore the circulation as he had hoped. On the surface he appeared self-confident and cool as ever and yet he was worried; Maggie knew him far too well not to know it.

With Beth safely transferred back to the unit, Pat and Bronwyn departed, promising a pot of tea for Maggie when she joined them. They would then probably sit round for an hour before going to bed, and often another case would come in while they were still up. To Maggie fell the task of writing up a brief report for the night supervisor; this done, she gave the theatre a last check over, then collected the box of morphine from the anaesthetic room. She thought Philip had left the unit, but she found him sitting at the office desk staring into space and looking intensely gloomy.

CHAPTER SIX

PHILIP dragged his hands down his face. God, he was tired! He saw Maggie standing in the doorway regarding him gravely with her enormous eyes, and his mouth twisted into a smile.

'All finished?' he asked gently, as she still hesitated. Tonight the lines of fatigue round his mouth and eyes bit deeply, and Maggie, all else forgotten, felt a tremendous surge of sympathy for this man who availed himself so freely for the benefit of others. 'Well, come in,' he said, his eyes amused; he leaned back in his chair watching her as she came forward. 'Beth come round yet?'

Maggie stood by the desk, the box in her hands. 'Only just. We checked her foot and she has a good strong pulse, and her toes are nice and pink and warm now . . .' When she had seen how cold and white they had been before the operation she had almost despaired that the circulation could ever be restored to normal. Even now she had a feeling it had been touch and go. Pondering, she absently smoothed the label back on the box where it was becoming unstuck.

'And . . . ?' Philip prompted. He watched her earnest young face and the long lowered lashes, suspecting she was deliberately avoiding his gaze, and that there was more to come.

Maggie hunched a shoulder uncertainly. 'Beth was in a terrible state for someone who'd been pre-medicated, don't you think?'

Philip nodded, 'Yes,' and his eyes dropped wearily to the notes in front of him. 'She thought she was going to lose her leg . . . and God knows, she might. For that eventuality I'll have to prepare her. Quite frankly, I don't know how I'm going to do it.'

How did one prepare another person for the loss of a limb? Maggie experimentally took one foot off the floor.

The false limbs they made these days were good, of course; she tried to imagine having something so cold and alien as part of her, unstrapping it that first time in front of someone new. Someone she loved and cared terribly what they thought. It was one thing to get used to a new body image—one's own—quite another for it to be accepted by others, and as Maggie knew from case histories, it sometimes never was. That was often the tragedy.

But one thing she did know, being incarcerated in the Intensive Care unit wasn't helping Beth to face up to reality. She stole a look at Philip, who had been too preoccupied to notice her wobbling about on one foot. 'Why not send her up to the orthopaedic ward with Sister Ferguson and her team—they've had a lot of experience in preparing and rehabilitating people like Beth.'

Philip grunted, paying scant attention to what was being said. Maggie pulled a resigned face and began over again. He stirred and frowned. 'I heard, and I'd rather not. Beth is better off in the unit. Besides, Sister Ferguson is a tyrant.'

'Maybe.' Maggie conceded the point reluctantly. 'But to the nurses, never to her patients. She gets very good results,' she added encouragingly, and Philip looked up from under his black brows.

'No . . . Beth needs careful monitoring. I can't possibly run the risk of someone failing to notice an arterial blockage, which as you know is not that apparent in the first stages.' Maggie picked up the box of morphine and fumbled for the drug cupboard keys in her pocket; she went for one more shot.

'It's terribly depressing in the unit—I mean, her nearest neighbour is in a coma, the next one is on a respirator and not exactly in any condition to be good company. And you must know yourself how dependent Beth is becoming on the nurses—physically and emotionally.'

Philip had arrived at that conclusion without any help from Maggie, and he suppressed a sigh. It wasn't that he blamed the ward staff. On nights there was often only one staff nurse, perhaps a couple of students if they were lucky. Could he expect her, with only the aid of a torch, to do a two-hourly check right through the night? If the first signs were missed, then it would be three, four, maybe five hours before something could be done about it.

With him reduced to staring blackly into space again Maggie thought it was time to change the subject. No surgeon appreciated a post-mortem on an operation he had only just completed; not anyway when it was the wee hours of the morning and the tail-end of a gruelling day.

'I've been meaning to ask about Tim . . .' And then she thought, damn, she was about to blunder into another hornets' nest. Oh well, she had started, she might as well finish. 'I hope you didn't send him straight back to school?'

Philip's eyebrows shot up.

'Now you're going to tell me how to bring up my son?' He saw her colour with embarrassment with a twinkle in his eye. The fact was, he had become more used to women hoping Tim *would* be at school than not. Maggie had fled to the cabinet with her box of drugs. He watched her sharply. 'How did you enjoy the charity do the other night? Duncan apparently took his brood along—he doesn't remember seeing you.'

'I didn't go, in fact I never really knew very much about it,' Maggie mumbled from the cupboard.

'Really?' Philip raised a quizzical brow. 'You had me fooled.' Then he laughed. 'Oh, but I admit it, I was a pompous ass, and I have to apologise. Tim explained everything. It was very nice of you to take him along and give him lunch. The thing was, being under the impression he was at his school, I was absolutely thrown.'

Maggie had turned and she was smiling. 'I can imagine.' Rather quickly she went back to her work and for a moment there was silence as she checked the drugs against what had been written up in the book. 'Is he all right now?' she asked. 'I phoned this morning.'

'You did?' The quick vibrant note of interest did not go unnoticed. Maggie pulled the door to, taking her time, not quite trusting herself to turn just yet and face him. When he was this nice, she couldn't find it in her to be angry with him, and she knew she must. It was her best defence. Already she was aware that this man could hurt her to a degree she had not thought possible.

'Oh,' she said, as casually offhand as it was possible to be, 'I thought Tim might have been at home, that's all.'

'As a matter of fact, he's staying with his grandmother for a few days. But then it's back to school and no nonsense.' Poor Tim, Maggie thought, though she imagined it would suit Claudia perfectly to be rid of the child—but eight years old seemed very young to be sent away to school. She still had her back to Philip when she heard the scrape of his chair as he got up. He was very close—too close.

'By the way, Tim gave me something for you.' Maggie turned and met his smiling blue eyes. 'It's in my jacket pocket, I'll get it later and leave it for you in my pigeonhole.'

'Thank you.' Maggie found she was suddenly quite breathless. He stood very tall in the small room, the harsh neon light glittered above his head—and suddenly she was afraid to look at him. Instead, she glanced up at the wall clock. 'Heavens, is that the time? I must go.'

She lifted her head to him as she passed; perhaps she had meant to say good night. But she would never know, for the words were never uttered. Philip's arms caught her and held her to him, and stood holding, knowing he was crazy and not caring. Maggie had become a soft pliable thing trembling against him, her head on his shoulder, her belly fitting snugly, his heart thudding against the upthrust of her breast, and neither of them knew who held whom. Then with a terrifying suddenness the bleep went off in his pocket, and Maggie jumped back the instant she was released, her heart beating wildly.

'Caught in the act?' There was the faintest hint of laughter in Philip's voice. 'That'll be the unit—I promised to go along. I expect they thought I'd skipped out on them.' Maggie nodded, her eyes rather desperately on the dark hairs showing in the V of his green cotton vest. What had happened just now between her and this . . . this man she hated?

Philip looked at the determined set of her small pointed chin, the milky opaque skin, the long concealing eyelashes, and longed to know what she was thinking. Would he ever? He wondered irrationally if she had ever worn pigtails when she was little. He turned away abruptly. 'Better get to bed while you have the chance, I've a feeling we might be busy later on.'

When she left, he was sitting easily on the desk, the telephone cradled between his chin and shoulder, ribbing the operator over some joke they had between them; Maggie could not imagine that he felt any of the bewilderment, or confusion, she felt, or that his life had been disturbed in any way.

Bronwyn's worried face peered down the stairs at her as she let herself in the door of the old East Wing. 'Heavens, Maggie, we were getting worried—tea's made.'

In the sitting-room Pat Mudie lay sprawled on a chintz-covered sofa that had seen better days; beside her on a low table was a tray with three mugs, a carton of milk and a plate of biscuits. The teapot nestled cosily in a cushion on the floor. Pat got herself in an upright position and picked it up. 'We thought you must have absconded with Philip Lonsdale,' she said, yawning.

Maggie snorted. 'He'd be the last person,' she declared, clinging to her battered self-deception.

Handing over a welcome mug of tea, Pat muttered, 'I'm glad someone's got some sense. It's bad enough these days, with Bronwyn going all moony over Gary!'

'Would you listen to her?' Bronwyn objected. 'When our new Charge can't keep her eyes off Philip Lonsdale's gorgeous body! Given half the chance I bet she'd eat him!'

It hurt. It hurt so much, Maggie closed her eyes briefly. Heaven help her if a few chance words spoken in jest were going to cause this much pain. She heard herself say, 'Claudia is beautiful, though. Those cool Swedish looks of hers.'

'So she might be, and with a profile to rival Garbo's, but she's as cold as a fish, make no mistake,' said Bronwyn, and Pat added darkly, 'Strange, isn't it, the way men go for that cool type. He'll marry her, wait and see.'

And what a fool she would be to imagine otherwise, Maggie thought, with something like despair and an ache she couldn't explain to herself if she had tried; she knew only that she had gone straight into Philip's arms that evening with the unerring instinct of a homing bird, as helplessly compelled as the arms that had reached out for her.

While the other two talked, Maggie settled back against a cushion with her feet tucked up by her side. She closed her eyes, feeling his arms go around her again, her mood turning dangerously warm and languid.

Of Philip she caught but a glimpse the next day, as he walked along the corridor deep in conversation with a doctor from the unit. The afternoon was busy, and once again Claudia had her rostered for another theatre. The hospital was quiet when she left at nine o'clock to go home. Jane pounced on her the moment she was in the front door, explaining in one long breath that they were giving a party for Fiona—who was apparently leaving almost immediately and more or less permanently for Australia.

'The party has to be tomorrow night,' said Jane, rattling off the details, 'because Fee leaves the morning after. And you're off duty at nine, and not on call back, so it'll be perfect.'

'Tomorrow night? What about food?' asked Maggie, taking a wild look about as if she hoped it would materialise out of thin air. But Jane was nothing if not organised. Nigel had promised to help, the girls would bring a dish of something, the men would bring wine. Then, promising Maggie she had something to show her, Jane ran off up the stairs humming.

'What *is* that tune?' Maggie asked Nigel, who had appeared from the kitchen.

'Love is the greatest thing . . . The oldest yet the latest thing . . .' Nigel crooned. She stared at him, then she was running up the stairs, taking them two at a time to arrive at Jane's doorway out of breath.

'Oh, Maggie . . .' Jane shoved out her hand and Maggie's startled gaze fell on the largest diamond she had ever seen. 'I met him the week you went home,' Jane told her, while Maggie sat on her bed and listened in astonishment. 'His name is Tom Gibson. He's a Canadian, his company makes surgical instruments. He had an appointment to see Paula, and I was waiting to see her myself, and we got talking . . .' Jane smiled, looking down at her ring.

'But, Jane,' Maggie protested, 'you've only known him a couple of weeks!'

'There, I knew you'd say that!' Jane said, her face taking on an obstinate look, but she went on when Maggie implored her to. 'Tom's a lot older than me, I'll admit,' adding with a quick sideways look, 'with a grown-up family and a daughter about my age. We want to get married in about six months and then I'll go to Canada with him.'

Maggie sat at her side on the bed. 'You always said you'd live in Canada!'

Afterwards they went downstairs where Nigel and Liv were scrambling eggs for a late supper, and then in the excitement of telling them, Maggie almost forgot the drawings Tim had done, and which Philip had left for her in his pigeonhole. 'Look,' she said, pulling them out of her bag.

Nigel leaned over. 'Lord, do I really look like that? No wonder his dad nearly flipped! When he comes tomorrow night I'd better have a couple of my specials, ready to soothe him down.'

It had never occurred to Maggie that Philip would

come. She said quickly to Jane, 'You didn't ask him, did you?'

'Of course we did,' Jane replied. 'He seems quite keen.'

Oh, Maggie could just imagine his look of polite interest. But not for one moment did she think he would actually come. Wild horses couldn't drag him to this house of iniquity. 'Don't count on it,' she managed from gritted teeth.

On duty the next afternoon Bronwyn was in a rebellious mood. 'She wants to go to Fee's party tonight,' Pat explained to Maggie. Pat and Bronwyn were both on call-back, along with Sue Manning who was resident in the nurses' home. Usually it was possible to swop round, if something came up at the last moment, but Claudia had put a stop to the practice. Now anyone wanting to change a duty had to give one week's notice.

'Maggie's place is less than five minutes away,' Bronwyn insisted. 'I can get the operator to call me if something comes in and be back in less than two. Oh, come on, it's done all the time, and you know it.'

'Not when I'm on,' Pat said grimly. 'And you're forgetting, Claudia will most likely be at the party herself. She'll go spare when she sees you there.'

'She won't even remember. Anyway, I don't care. If I get kicked out I'll go and get a job with decent pay and better hours.'

'Then you'd better get me one too, because I'll jolly well be thrown out with you,' Pat muttered with a baleful glare at Bronwyn's retreating back. 'Oh, don't go after her, Maggie, she's stubborn as a mule these days. I honestly think Gary has turned her head! With a bit of luck Claudia Fanslow won't put two and two together, if she notices at all.' They stared gloomily at the afternoon's list. 'Dr Technicolor Blakelock and his amazing tube ties again,' Pat muttered after a moment's silence.

The Gynae theatre went at its usual hectic pace and was followed on by a couple of acutes, but by the time nine o'clock came round the hospital was quiet and Bronwyn was excitedly showing off the dress she had bought especially for the party. 'I think I'll go over to Gary's and get dressed—he'll be surprised. He said I'd never have the nerve!' she laughed.

'I hope he's there, Bronny,' Pat said sceptically, and got a pitying smile in return.

'He is. Now don't panic, his flat is on the way to Maggie's. Ring there first if anything comes in.' Bronwyn packed the dress into a holdall and then, blowing them a kiss each, was off out the door.

'I don't know,' said Pat, 'I wouldn't be that certain of Gary, if it were me. But anyway, you go now, Maggie, if you want.'

Maggie shook her head. 'I'll stay on for ten or so minutes, there are a few things I have to attend to.' It troubled her that Pat had let Bronwyn get away with it: she never would have. But technically she was off duty now and it was one of those awkward situations where she couldn't do anything without treading on Pat's toes. Pat was in charge for the night hours—she was senior in years to Maggie and very jealous of her rank; it had been enough that Maggie had been promoted to acting charge when Fiona was off sick.

Just as she was about to leave the phone rang. Maggie was in the office and answered it herself. Alec Blakelock was on the line. 'Maggie—we've got a ruptured ectopic pregnancy in Cas,' he told her.

It was one of those rare instances when there wasn't five minutes to spare in which to get organised; they had a surgical emergency on their hands. Maggie gave Pat the details. 'I'll go and get set up, you ring for Bronwyn and Sue.' She left her dialling Gary's number and muttering dire threats.

Maggie was throwing crates and packs on to a trolley when Pat came in, tying her mask. 'Sue's coming and I can't get any answer from Gary and neither of them are at your place yet—I could kick myself! What in hell are we to do?'

Maggie shoved a laparotomy pack into her hands as she saw Fred Jenkins, the consultant gynaecologist, coming down the corridor. 'Get Sue to do the anaesthetic side and I'll stay on—I'll have to. We haven't a moment to lose.'

'Oh, Maggie, be a dear, would you scrub? I'm all thumbs with Fred when he's in a hurry.'

'Sure—though it'll cost you,' grinned Maggie, then she was off. On her way she looked in on the anaesthetic room and was relieved to find Sue there already and looking quite at home. Maggie couldn't wait for the patient to arrive and hurried on.

In the scrubroom Fred Jenkins' tall frame was stooped over the sink. He was wearing his white rubber boots —he thought clogs were some kind of fashion trend invented by halfwits. 'Good evening, Sister Bell, patient here?'

'Hasn't arrived yet, sir.' Maggie wisely took the sink furthest away; Fred was one of those surgeons who managed to splash water over everything nearby in the process of scrubbing his arms.

'Beautiful young woman, prime of life. Gone to all kinds of trouble trying to conceive.' He sighed deeply, and Maggie wondered if he was thinking about the list of tubal ligations they had done that afternoon. 'Where's young Blakelock?' he barked suddenly.

As though on cue, Alec came through the door. He rolled his eyes in Maggie's direction and stationed himself deferentially next to the consultant, prepared to endure the splashes: he was hoping to keep his job for another term.

The patient, when she appeared in theatre, was in shock and the minutes counted; Maggie and Alec worked furiously to get her draped, while Fred tapped his gloved fingers together, his eyes on the sphygmomanometer dial. They waited a few minutes for the anaesthetist to get the patient stable, but he was looking worried and Fred was forced to start: the only treatment in this case being to remove the cause of the shock.

Maggie was ready, she slapped the scalpel into his hand and he made his incision, skin and muscles were drawn aside and held securely open by retractors, a well of blood oozed up and had to be sucked away. The tension was almost palpable. Fred's forehead glistened under the lights as he worked, his gloved hands moving fast and always outstretched, it seemed to Maggie, for more and yet more instruments.

Fifteen minutes later he was on the way out, and Maggie nodded to Pat for a count before he closed the peritoneum. Fred wasn't a man to hang round. Pat had been rushing about like a mad thing trying to keep up with their incessant demands, and her face was beetroot-red.

'Intensive care for the night—can you arrange it, Sister, please.' He looked up with a pleasant smile. 'What do you think eh? One good Fallopian tube left. I'd say she has a fifty-fifty chance of being able to bring a baby to full term—let's hope so.' Peeling off his gloves, he nodded his thanks to them and left Alec to finish closing the skin.

'How did you like the anaesthetic side?' Maggie asked Sue as she closed the doors to the unit after their patient had been safely handed over.

'Much better,' Sue said.

They walked back to the theatres together. Pat met them in the corridor. 'I'll wring Bronwyn's neck for her!' She paused. 'In fact, I'm going to do that now.'

'Is she back?' asked Maggie in surprise, and Pat said, glowering, 'No—but she will be. I'm going to phone now.' As she was speaking, they heard the office phone ring. Pat crossed her fingers and went to answer it. Maggie followed her along and sat by the desk while she took the details.

'They've just brought in a young woman—suspected fractures both legs. She's been knocked down by a cab not far from here . . .' Pat looked up, startled, as Gary appeared at the doorway, and it flashed through Maggie's mind that something was terribly wrong. But Pat was more concerned with Bronwyn's whereabouts than Gary's glassy-eyed appearance. 'I tried to ring you earlier on.' Her voice was accusing.

'Was that you? I wish to hell I had answered it now.' His boyishly handsome face had aged ten years, and he seemed lost; Maggie stared at him with growing alarm. Suddenly he said, 'I had no idea she was coming over—we'd planned on going to the party, I wasn't on call—I thought she might have showed up for ten minutes or so, but not at my place.'

Maggie stood up and gripped his arm. 'That girl in Cas?' He nodded, and she heard Pat's, 'Oh, my God!'

'There's no time now for explanations,' Gary said roughly. 'She needs a good surgeon. Lonsdale's the best, but I can't get hold of him. Can you try while I get hold of her parents, then I'll get changed.'

'But he's not on call tonight, I can't . . .'

Gary cut in on Pat.

'Get him. He'll come, I know it.' Pat took a step back, her face white, but she was on the phone before he left the room.

'He's not answering. I'll try this other number here.' Pat started dialling again. 'You know Gary has this little nurse in Recovery on the string as well,' she said to Maggie. 'I've never liked him, not from the first day he poked his smarmy nose round the door. Damn it, why is it no one is answering tonight?'

'Pat,' said Maggie, 'it'll be a while before we can get organised, I'm going round to see her—I won't be more than five minutes.'

The corridors were quiet, here and there a night nurse on some errand, or going to an early supper, the odd visitor leaving late. Maggie pushed open the swing doors of the casualty department and hurried along the passage between the curtained cubicles towards the group of doctors and nurses at the end. As she approached, the Casualty Registrar stepped her way. 'Hello,' he smiled, recognising her. 'Sister Bell, isn't it?' At Maggie's nod, he said, 'You can go in and see her. She's conscious but not in pain at the moment—we've given her a fair whack of morphine.' He stood aside and pulled back a curtain. 'It's all right, nurse, you can leave her with Sister Bell for the moment,' and Maggie went in.

Bronwyn turned her head listlessly. Her eyes were open, they flickered aimlessly; she seemed not to recognise Maggie. 'Bronny,' Maggie whispered, 'it's me.'

Slowly the pupils focused and the white lips formed a smile. 'Maggie . . .'

'Don't talk, Bron. I just came along to see you. Gary told us.' Bronwyn turned her head away and Maggie had to lean right over to catch her words.

'I don't want to see him, ever again.' Maggie straightened slowly as the doctor came back in.

Philip came through the Casualty doors as Maggie was leaving Bronwyn's cubicle; her pensive face and strained mouth told him all he needed to know. 'You were supposed to be off hours ago,' he said, going up to her.

'That hardly matters,' she said quietly. Did he imagine a gentle reproof? He had the impression then that she was much older than her years, and had to remind himself that she was only twenty-two.

'Brad is parking the car, he'll be with us in a moment,' he told her. Maggie nodded. It didn't seem so strange that Alan should come in, he thought a lot of Bronwyn. 'Duncan too—he's on his way. Do you know where Gary is?'

'He was going to try and get in touch with her parents, and then get changed,' she told him, watching the curtains part as the nurses came and went from Bronwyn's bedside. Yet already she wasn't quite as worried for her. The mere fact that Philip had come, and would do everything humanly possible, was enough to allay her worst fears.

Philip reached his arm out and took her lightly by the elbow. 'I want you to go round and ask Gary to wait for me in my office while I examine Bronwyn. He's far too emotionally involved to assist with this operation.' He studied her face and she looked gravely back at him. 'Can you scrub and assist me?'

'Of course.' Philip smiled and nodded. Maggie had more grit than others twice her size. And he could rely on her to get everything perfectly organised in her own calm way, this paradox that was Maggie. For an instant he watched her go, then he turned, nodding briskly to the Casualty Sister, then the two of them went in to see Bronwyn.

Midnight had gone before they were finished. Gary waited in the corridor as they eased Bronwyn's cumbersome orthopaedic bed through the doorway. Little of his old self remained and he had the glazed look of a man waking from a nightmare. Maggie felt desperately sorry for him, though she knew little yet of what had actually taken place.

Philip emerged from the theatre discarding mask, gloves and cap on his way. 'She's going to be fine,' he said, smiling. 'We managed to achieve a good bone union, a few weeks in traction, of course—there's a side room up in Sister Ferguson's ward, should do nicely. You might like to sit with her until she wakes up.'

Maggie held her tongue. Bronwyn might have said she didn't want to see Gary again—she might not have meant it. Somehow Maggie suspected she would appreciate a hand to hold when she came round. 'I'd like to,' Gary said, and he looked as though he meant it.

'Good—good,' Alan Bradford said cheerfully. 'Then you can take Maggie's place and help push this thing. The porters have decided to air one of their many grievances, so unless we take the bed up ourselves Brownwyn will be spending the night in the corridor.'

'Scoot,' ordered Pat, 'before the phone goes again.' Maggie was only too pleased to scoot. Philip had insisted on calling in extra staff, so there was no shortage of hands to do the cleaning up, and one of the nurses living in was to take the rest of the night's call duty in Bronwyn's place. She went along to the office to sign for her extra hours and found Philip studying the next day's operating schedule. He looked round as she came in.

'Tired?' he asked.

She nodded. She couldn't remember the last time she had been so tired, or for that matter, the last time she had eaten anything solid. 'And hungry,' she added, remembering the delicious things there would be at home. The party would be nearly over now. She looked at him uncertainly, wondering if she dared invite him.

But she hesitated. People would have gone home by now, it being a week night. Nigel's crowd on the other hand would be getting wound up, and she wasn't in a mood for their particular brand of hilarity.

'Going by the way people were devouring everything in sight, there won't be much left to eat at your place,' Philip said unexpectedly, and almost smiled at her look of astonishment. Perhaps she thought he was too stuffy to go to parties. 'Fortunately I have a well stocked fridge at home.'

Was he asking her to supper? Maggie blushed furiously, wishing she had kept her mouth shut. 'Well, what do you say?' he asked quizzically.

'Oh,' Maggie panicked, 'but it's a bit late, don't you think?'

Philip laughed—this was rich coming from Maggie! He would have thought it her usual supper time. He grinned wickedly. 'I'm asking you home for a meal, and I wasn't thinking of taking no for an answer!'

Philip's flat came as a surprise; Maggie had somehow imagined something austere, spartan. It was neither. She followed him through a long booklined hallway and into a spacious room full of comfortable chairs, reading lamps and paintings. A long low table was drawn up to a cushioned sofa, and it seemed not to matter that the floor was strewn with magazines and papers, or that the windows were crowded with a tangled mass of geraniums. 'Bit of a mess,' he said ruefully, though he didn't sound if he cared in the least as he led her on through to the kitchen, which by comparison looked very tidy.

Any stiffness Maggie might have felt was soon dissipated as Philip collected a bottle of wine and glasses and talked amiably about matters of mutual interest. When he had assembled an assortment of food on the bench, he asked, 'Think this lot can be turned into a passable omelette?'

Maggie thought so, and was quite prepared to set to work. She picked up the egg beater, and was promptly swept back to the living room, shown the stereo system and selection of records, given directions for the bathroom if required, then left to relax with her glass of wine.

Somewhat abstracted, she selected a favourite old blues record, put it on the turntable, then gingerly sat down on the sofa. As she sipped, her bones seemed to dissolve into the soft downy cushions; a delicious feeling of languor stole over her and she abandoned herself to the luxury of complete relaxation.

They ate their supper by candlelight, sitting on either side of the long low table. Maggie couldn't remember when an omelette had tasted so delicious. 'Coffee?' asked Philip, when they had finished and she had heard about Tim's subsequent return to school, and that he was settling down again more or less contentedly. She shook her head. 'Then a little more wine.' He topped up her glass and settled the bottle back in its container.

'You talked to Gary. Did he tell you what happened?' she asked.

For a long moment Philip studied the wine in his glass, then at last he said, 'Only that she came up to his flat when he wasn't expecting her. He wasn't alone, you see.' Maggie closed her eyes, it was what she had thought must have happened. 'He opened the door to her in his bathrobe—— Gary didn't elaborate, but I take it he had another girl in his bed. It must have been quite a shock for Bronwyn.'

Maggie remembered Bronwyn's radiant face as she had danced in her new dress a few short hours ago. Would she ever again? Maggie wondered. Philip sighed. 'Mind if I smoke?' and she shook her head in surprise. His smile was weary. 'A cigar after dinner sometimes, that's all. Helps me to relax.'

He stood up and went to the mantelpiece, taking a cigar from a box. Instead of coming back to sit down, he stayed where he was to light it. Maggie, watching him, thought how strangely the evening had turned out, so different from how it had been planned. Poor dear Bronny . . . Philip startled her by saying, 'Tim never showed me his drawings, you know, the ones he did for you.'

'Oh,' she said, 'they're up on our fridge.'

'I know—Nigel showed me,' he chuckled richly. 'I thought they were very good, an amazing likeness to Nigel.' His dark eyes sought hers. 'You thought I wouldn't go to the party.'

'Do you blame me?' said Maggie, her cheeks dimpling, then a thought crossed her mind. 'Claudia,' she said suddenly. 'Was Claudia there?' Philip knew from the anxious note in her voice, or thought he did, what was going through her mind.

'Bronwyn was going to the party, wasn't she? Did she ask you to change duties with her?' He watched her hesitate, the long eyelashes flicker as she half looked at him.

'Is that what Claudia thinks?' was Maggie's guarded response.

He shook his head. 'Claudia wasn't at the party, and my guess is that she knows nothing about the accident yet.' He had pretty well worked out what had happened, and he guessed Maggie was covering up for Bronwyn.

'Well, I expect she'll find out soon enough,' Maggie said with beguiling candour. 'Did you get a chance to talk to Fee? I believe she's leaving for Heathrow early in the morning.' She looked at him with her large clear eyes; Philip was half amused. He had wondered, even expected, she would ask his help in keeping Claudia off the scent, but she hadn't—and wasn't going to, apparently. Perhaps she didn't trust him. The thought annoyed him.

'Fiona is in fine fettle, and yes, I managed a word or two.' He walked over to the cabinet and poured two small glasses of cognac. Returning to the sofa, he replaced her half-finished wine with the brandy glass, then he took his own glass and slumped back in his chair, taking a meditative sip.

'Jane is engaged—did you meet her fiancé?' asked Maggie, sensing his change of mood and striving to keep the conversation going on subjects she felt safe with.

'Yes—nice sort. I liked him.' Silence. Maggie took a sip of cognac and felt the fire take hold of her throat and then spread through her body. Philip puffed on his cigar. He tilted his head back and breathed out the smoke, his eyes hooded. 'Why didn't you tell me you'd broken off your engagement?'

His voice was gentle—soothing, like the cognac. There was nothing dangerous about it. Oh, but if only he knew how much she had wanted to tell him, that night he had come with the daffodils. But how could she? He would only have thought her fickle. And then that night in the restaurant . . . She took another sip; everything seemed very clear and still, the cognac in her stomach warm and wonderful, spreading its protection like a silky blanket.

She looked up at him, her eyes searching. 'I could never reach you to make you understand . . .'

'Understand what, Maggie?' Philip's voice was very gentle. She heard him move in his chair, then cross the short space between them. Her heart bumped wildly, the glass in her hand shook; he took it from her and his lips came slowly down on hers, his fingers reaching into the tangle of hair at the back of her neck.

For a breath, she held her mouth closed, and then slowly her lips parted and she hung on to his mouth for timeless moments while his tongue probed and possessed her. As his hands moved the ache in her body became an exquisite torment, she had waited a lifetime for this: her mouth on his, her arms around him.

He had kissed her without thought, and now he couldn't stop. His impassioned body drove him on, and he groaned, his fingers caressing her breasts to hard peaks. He ripped his shirt open and pressed her against him, her skin under his hands; she was melting against him, responding to him in a way that aroused him to fever pitch.

And then, in some detached corner of his brain—a surgeon's brain—reality overcame his drowning senses, and he pulled back. He knew that if he didn't get up and walk away now, he would weaken, and he wouldn't be able to stop. The consequences would be disastrous for them both.

'Maggie . . .' Her hair was a wild mass of curls, her grey eyes trusting; Philip closed his eyes and held her tight against him. 'Maggie,' he breathed, 'I must take you home. We're both very tired, and tomorrow there's work to do as usual.'

Fifteen minutes later he was seeing her in the front door of her house. He bent his head to kiss her good night, intending only a warm farewell. She stood on tiptoe, raising her arms to encircle his neck.

'Oh, Maggie, Maggie . . .' He held on to her for precious moments, as if frightened of ever letting go, then gently he unwound her arms.

Back in his flat he poured a large brandy. Useless to tell himself she was too young and unsettled to take on the burden of mothering an eight-year-old boy. He needed her. He thought sometimes he would go crazy if he couldn't have her.

Philip flung himself full length down on the sofa on which Maggie's scent still lingered. He took the brandy in one gulp and then reminded himself that he needed to fall in love with a pretty young party girl, the image of his first wife, like he needed a hole in the head.

CHAPTER SEVEN

HALF HAPPY and half miserable, Maggie was lost in too many difficult thoughts to notice her fellow passengers on the underground journey to Heathrow the following morning. Nobody and nothing had prepared her for being in love—truly in love; the ups and downs, the joy, the sheer misery of it. As she stared at the passing scenery she thought it hardly seemed possible such closeness could exist between two people as she had experienced in that long kiss. But even that detail scarcely conveyed her feelings, or the magic that had shifted the whole world on its axis. That it had not been the same for Philip was unthinkable.

Fiona was at the check-in counter haggling over the amount of in-flight luggage allowed on board when Maggie eventually caught up with her. 'Quite ridiculous,' Fee said. 'What's one or two wee bags going to hurt?'

'Fee . . .' Maggie offered the crisp young woman behind the counter a conciliatory smile, and hissed back, 'You can't take all that stuff on with you—at least check the overnight bags.' Fiona sighed, but did as Maggie advised and heaved the offending bags on to the scales. The people in the queue behind shuffled with impatience, but at last Fiona had her seat number and boarding cards, and they were able to go in search of coffee.

'Great party last night.' Fiona ruefully eased into one of the lurid green plastic chairs with a sigh.

'Oh, I'm glad. Was it fun, then?' Maggie asked, having had little opportunity to find out, in the early morning scramble to see Fiona off; though if the state of the house was anything to go by, the party had been a huge success.

'Your Nigel was fun,' Fiona claimed, blissfully unaware of Maggie's quick frown. 'You know hospital people and their incessant shop talk . . .' She proceeded to fill in the details, and Maggie gathered that Nigel had done some of his impressions. She bit her lip—some of those she had seen!

'Nothing in drag, I hope?' she asked.

'Don't think so,' Fiona said blandly. 'After he did his Bondi Beach thing . . . How does he get a tan like that in this climate?'

'Sun-bed,' Maggie said briefly.

'Very sensible—oh well, after he did that, he made me a couple of specials, rum punches I think they were, and I've no idea what happened after that.' Maggie raised an eyebrow: Fee was quite capable of drinking the best of them under the table, and usually did on such occasions, and she always remained as sober as a judge to the end. More likely, Fee was censoring some of the details, Maggie thought, and her suspicion was confirmed when Fiona winked with sombre good humour and then suddenly became serious.

'I phoned the hospital this morning,' she said. 'Bronwyn's fine, a bit uncomfortable, as you would expect with two smashed legs. Philip did a nice job —though I don't have to tell you that. Poor kid, it's a damned shame.' And then she railed on about doctors. 'Young tykes,' she grumbled. 'Not that youth has anything to do with it, mind you. The older ones are just as good at breaking hearts. They seem to have a natural proclivity for it.'

Maggie, squirming in her seat, prodded at the sticky bun Fiona had insisted on buying. 'I think Gary might be in love with her,' she said. 'You know, Fee, he was very upset last night.'

'Well yes, he would be, though. It's a very upsetting business all round.' Fiona sighed. 'Strange, isn't it, everyone else knew he was seeing this other nurse . . . But it's always the way. Oh, but I hope you're right and that he does stick by her. Here, Maggie, you have my Danish. Whatever possessed me, after the amount I ate last night? Shame you missed out on the party, Jane so wanted to introduce Tom to you. You'll meet him tomorrow night, though, I expect.'

'Tomorrow night?' Maggie echoed blankly, then remembered the promotion party Tom's company was putting on for all theatre personnel. 'What *is* he like, Fee?' she asked curiously.

'He's a love. I'd fancy him myself, I really would. The nicest brown eyes. Big smile, like he meant it. Jane's in her element. But I've always said she's one of those girls who looks undressed without a baby or two in her arms and a man to fuss over. And she's quite happy now that she's given up worrying about him being so much older. She came to see me; just wanted a wee talk before finally saying the word.'

'Oh.' Maggie stirred her coffee, nursing a sense of disappointment. Jane and she had been friends for years, and she felt rather hurt not to have been confided in first. She shrugged. 'Well, I guess she didn't want to ask my opinion. You see, my father is probably getting married to a girl young enough to be my sister, and I suppose I might have said something . . .' As she was speaking the flight information screen whirred over with new digits and they both glanced up.

'That's my flight.' Fiona began gathering up her bits and pieces, but suddenly she stopped, looking at Maggie. 'Oh, there's so much I wanted to talk about, and now there isn't time. But you are happy, dear . . . now that you've made your decision to break with John?'

John? Maggie shook her curly head. 'Fee, I loved him, but I wasn't in love. At the time I never knew the difference. It's taken——' she was going to say Philip and bit his name back just in time, '—well, it's taken a broken engagement to find out,' she finished somewhat lamely.

'You deserve to meet someone nice, and you will —and Maggie, I did enjoy the party so much, and please tell Jane. I'll be writing, of course. Oh, but I shall miss you all! And now I'd better go, or heaven help me, I shall be crying all over the place.'

When Maggie saw the straight back of Fiona's brisk

little figure disappearing through the departures door she felt like having a good weep herself. Fiona had taught her all she knew about working in an operating theatre, and a lot more besides. She had been strict, but fair, and she was going to be sorely missed.

'What is the rate of success in the surgical procedure I'm doing?' Philip Lonsdale asked, and a brash young medical student piped up from the back of the group.

'A sympathectomy is successful only in those patients . . . er . . . in whom the vessels are still elastic enough to dilate,' he told the surgeon confidently, improvising from the notes he had hidden beside him.

'Very good,' Philip said with a hint of sarcasm that went right past the young man. 'But next time place your textbook out where others may gain the benefit from it.' There was a titter of amusement from the appreciative students.

'. . . 5-0 silk,' Philip murmured. He extended his hand for the needle-holder Maggie had ready and then set to work, closing up the wound with fine neat sutures; the students moved closer, admiring the beautiful precision of his work. The afternoon had been a series of fairly short cases and Philip had performed with his usual patience and skill, and he was, as always, working against the clock in an effort to get to his evening lectures in time.

He raised his eyes, the corners crinkling in a smile above his mask as he handed the instrument back to Maggie. Then he glanced up at the wall clock and grimaced, because he was running late and he hated to keep his students waiting. It was a usual kind of afternoon. Nothing out of the ordinary had happened.

That was the trouble. Maggie had expected it would be—well, different in some way—oh, she didn't know in what way, but something. Some secret sign, some message that he knew and understood how she felt, because it was the same for him and that he couldn't wait for their next meeting when they could be alone.

Not this stultifying sameness—as if the night before

had never happened. There had been no whispered exchange, nothing that could not have been heard by the others . . . But she was being silly. Of course he would want to keep their professional relationship just that: absolutely separate. That way there would be no gossip, and Maggie could only be grateful to him for that.

She was just as grateful to find Claudia on her day off, as she had rather feared an inquisition into Bronwyn's untimely accident. Or more precisely, the fact that Bronwyn had not been on hospital premises when it happened. Paula Crisp in a quiet word had intimated her disapproval of on-call staff being anywhere other than in the quarters provided for them. But she had, in the circumstances, declined to act further. In theatre, where yesterday's news got forgotten in the drama of the moment, Maggie hoped the matter would die a natural death before Claudia returned—though her own uneasiness about the situation continued to plague her.

Jane was on with her for call-back that night, and after they had cleared a backlog of acutes, both girls went up to visit Bronwyn. They found her rather too drowsy to talk much, but happy to have company. A little later on Gary joined them, sheepishly clutching a huge bouquet of roses; for a while they talked, sitting round the bed, then Jane and Maggie left.

'I hope they can work it out,' said Maggie as she settled down by the phone in the night quarters. 'And they might, given half a chance, and without the sort of comments Alec Blakelock was making. Did you hear him in the café this evening, going on about hysterical birds jumping to wild conclusions? I felt like throwing some of my meatballs at him—they're as hard as rocks anyway. Wish I had now!'

'I was in two minds whether to hit him myself, on principle,' Jane agreed, then added thoughtfully, 'Though I'm not sure I'd lose my head over a man enough to get me run down in the street.'

'Oooh,' Maggie flashed her an enquiring look, 'not even Tom? Come on, if you arrived unexpectedly at his flat and found him in the arms of another girl? Come on,' she said encouragingly, as Jane hesitated.

'Well, I'd be mad,' she admitted, 'but Tom . . . ? Oh, Maggie, you can't imagine how shy he is—why, I had to ask him out!' Her face flamed with colour. 'And so help me, Maggie Bell, if you ever so much as breathe a word to a soul!'

The phone rang and Maggie jumped. She picked it up, her heart in her mouth; a voice with an American accent asked for Jane and she smiled, hiding her disappointment. 'It's for you, Jane, I think it must be Tom.'

They waited until midnight, then Maggie rang the operator to check if the hospital was quiet. It was, and they decided to go to bed. Jane yawned and stretched. 'I hope it stays quiet, I want to look reasonably gorgeous for the party tomorrow night. Tom said he'd send a cab for you, say about nine-thirty—you can make it later if you think that doesn't give you enough time to get home and get ready.'

Maggie lay awake a long time. She had thought Philip might have called. But maybe he had been busy with his lectures, maybe even stayed late to mark papers; she told herself that he often went out for a drink with his students, and probably that he hadn't even arrived home yet. Not entirely convinced, she at last rolled over and went to sleep.

When the phone did ring, it was Gary on the line. 'Maggie, that you?' he asked as she mumbled her name. 'You sound weird . . .' As if anybody wouldn't at five-thirty in the morning, Maggie thought, checking her watch.

'We have a young man in Cas with stab wounds. He must have put out his arm to defend himself, because it's pretty chopped up. I've called Lonsdale. Think you'd like to get your team together and slip over, give us a hand?'

Maggie stopped only to splash her face with cold water and pull a white coat on over her pyjamas, then she roused Jane and Sue and went on ahead. It was five-forty exactly when she turned into the hospital corridor that led to the operating theatres; she was hurrying, her mind preoccupied with what she had to do when she got there. In passing, she caught a glimpse of a car through the window, pulling into the parking space outside. It was not a car she recognised.

Absently she glanced out at the next window, this time noticing the woman sitting at the driving wheel. Then the passenger door opened, and Maggie froze in her stride as she saw Philip climb out. Paralysed, she watched him walk round to the driver's side. The curtain of blonde hair that had obscured the woman's profile fell away as she raised her face to him.

'Good heavens!' exclaimed Jane said, coming up behind her. 'That's Claudia Fanslow. Well, well, well, so she's managed to hook him after all!'

Maggie shivered. It was too much to take in—but in that one hideous moment she knew why Bronwyn had plunged recklessly, blindly out into the road.

They walked on, Jane unaware that Maggie looked alarmingly ashen and grave, fearful, and she chattered blithely on. Imprinted in Maggie's mind, with all the intensity of an old black and white photograph, was a picture of that pale upturned expectant face—and Philip's dark head as he bent down. Had he kissed her? Why not? Presumably he had spent the night with Claudia. What else could she think?

'We'll be needing the three-pronged muscle retractors . . .' Maggie had followed Philip into the scrub room and they were both starting their five-minute wash. Under the stark neon lights the room had a strange surreal quality that was not noticeable during the daylight hours. Her mouth felt gritty, and she had an awful nauseous feeling in her stomach, as though she might at any moment be sick.

She replied, 'We have everything you want . . . sir.' Something in her voice caused Philip to turn his head in a long hard look, but her profile told him nothing. The clean proud beauty of her body was somehow heightened by the chaste line of her plain cotton dress; only too conscious of the effect she was having on him, Philip turned back to scrubbing his arms.

'What a time to pick a fight,' he said gruffly. 'It looks as if someone took a carving knife to that young man!' He glanced back at Maggie and saw the corners of her beautiful mouth turn down.

She had seen the man—and the punctured arm lying uselessly by his side congealing in its own blood. Philip, glancing at her again, thought it best to change the subject. At this time of the morning even the hardest of stomachs could turn on one.

'I got a card from Tim yesterday,' he said conversationally. 'He'd painted it himself in art class. Next thing I suppose he'll want to be an artist. He asked after you.'

Maggie smiled slightly when she heard that, but kept her gaze downcast. She did not trust her eyes to meet his, however briefly, in case they should reveal too much. She said nothing, and Philip resisted the impulse to sigh. It wasn't going to be easy, getting her out of his system. He had to, of course. There was his son to consider. He should be thinking of marrying a woman nearer his own age, yet instead here he was yearning for this child beside him; he thought how much he wanted to press his lips to the pulse that throbbed at the base of her creamy throat, and nearly groaned.

He shoved the tap off with his elbow; it was time to put aside such thoughts. Unbeknown to him, Maggie was having to do the same. It was important, and not everybody was capable of it. But the two of them shared a professionalism and a confidence that was almost tangible, it was something their private world never intruded upon.

The patient was strapped down on the table, shoulders braced, in case they might have to wind it into the Trendelenburg position: lowering his upper body and head to the bottom of as steep an incline as necessary to cope with surgical shock. Philip was talking quietly to Gary, and Maggie stood a little apart as the three waited for the anaesthetist's signal to begin draping.

As they waited, the scrub doors swung open and a laboratory technician shuffled through in gown and overshoes, tying his mask. Maggie glanced towards the group working round the table; Jane was busy, so she went over herself to where the technician was waiting.

'We've cross-matched a couple of units, they're in your fridge.' Maggie nodded her thanks. His eyes shifted rapidly to the patient lying anaesthetised on the table, and back to Maggie.

'We're also doing a check for serum hepatitis. He's a registered drug addict.'

Maggie had expected as much from the marks on the man's uninjured arm, and from his ankles; she had seen to it that the rest of the team, not gowned and gloved, were suitably protected with disposable clothing as a precautionary measure. It had not been so long since a theatre nurse had died through having contracted the disease.

The technician slipped away, his business finished, but Maggie stood a moment, preoccupied with her thoughts. Serum hepatitis was a very real danger. Occurring often in drug addicts who had infected themselves with contaminated needles, it could then be transmitted to anyone who came in contact with the infected blood.

The procedure for isolating the staff against becoming infected was complicated—a headache. Claudia would be tearing her hair out when she came on, for the theatre would have to be closed for anything up to twenty-four hours, which meant the day's list being completely disrupted. Some cases could still be done in other theatres, others would have to be cancelled. Claudia . . . The name left a bitter taste on Maggie's lips.

She was about to walk back and join the others when the sound of the door opening to the scrub room made her look round. At first she thought the lab technician had returned; she soon realised he was not the same man, for all that he was concealed by cap, mask and long bulky gown. It did occur to her as being odd, because the hospital only ever called in one person at a time to do the out-of-hours laboratory work. Unless they were very busy, which they weren't, as far as Maggie knew.

She took a step forward, barring his way into the theatre itself. It was an instinctive reaction, and something she couldn't explain later on. His eyes went past her to the unconscious man on the table, and then they were on Maggie in a wild drug-crazed stare. For a split second they faced each other, Maggie's mouth drying with horror as she realised he carried a flick-knife in his hand.

He lunged, but she was quicker, catching him a glancing blow on the shins with her heavy clog. 'Look out!' she screamed. 'He's got a knife!'

The man twisted in a menacing snake-like movement and lashed out at her, his lips bared from his teeth. She flattened herself back against the wall and felt the knife rip through the sleeve of her gown and pierce her wrist. Under her terrified gaze, he pitched slowly forward. Her mouth was open to scream again when she saw that Philip had brought him down in a flying tackle. There was a shortlived struggle on the floor, then her assailant was being dragged to his feet and frogmarched out the door by Gary and a frightened-looking little medical student who had been on hand to watch the operation.

Maggie was only vaguely aware of the blood staining her gown bright red; the fact that two of the theatre staff were walking through the hospital in clothing that could be contaminated worried her very much more. She started to tell Philip, who was beside her, and was surprised when she began to slide down the wall.

'I'm all right,' she gasped as he whipped her off her feet. 'It's only a little nick,' but she was talking to the hard obstinate line of his jaw and she knew she might as well save her breath. Jane hurried ahead of them and flung open the doors to the anaesthetic room. The moment Maggie was on the recovery trolley, Philip slapped a pad on her wound and pressed tightly.

'The patient,' she said desperately. 'May have serum hepatitis...' Philip swore under his breath. That was all they needed! He told Jane to go and phone the lab and find out for sure.

'And leave your outer things this side of the door. Warn the others, and re-gown when you come back in.' When the bleeding had stopped, he ripped off the sleeve from Maggie's gown. 'Aha!' he exclaimed, when he saw the wound. 'Doesn't look much, but it could be deep —that's the trouble with these pierce-type injuries. It needs a couple of stitches, we'll do it now.'

'But the patient?' Maggie asked. 'The patient is fine,' Philip told her. 'We have his bleeding under control —you're the one haemorrhaging! Now lie back and keep that arm up while I go and re-glove. It won't take us more than a few minutes.'

'Next time, dive for cover,' Jane told her severely, when she got back. 'Whatever made you think you could stop one of those fiends? It's a wonder he didn't cream you!'

'Oh, thanks very much,' muttered Maggie, but feeling a lot better now she was lying down. The anaesthetist came and prodded her arm, injecting some lignocaine around the wound.

'That should do the trick,' he said cheerfully, then returned to his patient, leaving Jane to swab her arm with iodine.

'It's my wrist,' Maggie protested, as Jane seemed bent on painting her yellow.

'Can't be too careful, dear,' Jane murmured, and Philip, arriving with a suture set, smiled behind his mask.

It was curious, not being able to feel Philip's deft fingers as he probed and aligned, and Maggie wondered coldly what pleasure those same strong gentle hands had brought to Claudia during the night. When he had finished she sat up, prepared to slip down from the high trolley.

'Where do you think you're going?' he asked.

'Back to work,' she said, surprised by his gruffness, and feeling a little foolish about all this trouble over a small injury when their patient had far worse.

'The devil you are! They're waiting for you in Casualty. You need a few shots, young lady. Afterwards, I'll have someone drive you home. You'd better get to bed and stay there for the next twenty-four hours.'

'But . . .' Maggie protested feebly, suddenly feeling

rather less strong now that she was in an upright position. 'What about . . .?'

Philip, looking indulgently down at her, grunted, 'See that she behaves,' and left the room.

'Yes, sir,' said Jane, staring after him. 'That man is becoming positively human, I swear! Now listen—don't you worry, we'll see everything is done by the book, if it makes you any happier. And don't forget, you have the next two days off in any case. We'll get someone to work your duty this afternoon, so don't worry about that either.' She hurried about the room as she talked, stuffing the used linen into yellow bags and tidying as she went.

Redundant, Maggie watched, and resigned herself to the inevitable. Then the porter arrived to take her to Casualty and within minutes she was in a chair being wheeled along the eerily quiet corridors, listening with genuine bemusement to a somewhat highly coloured version of what had just taken place.

It was late afternoon when she woke from sleep crying, choking with sobs and with a dull heavy ache in her chest. 'Oh, Philip,' she whispered, 'you made me love you. What a fool I am!'

The room was stifling. Unmindful of her fuzzy head and bandaged arm, she heaved herself out of bed and went to open the windows. It was a perfect spring day outside, the light mellow and golden. When had the trees become green, she wondered, the roses in bud? How could it all be so lovely, when she felt so bleak and grey and cold?

She had not seen the anguish in Philip's eyes as he rushed to her aid. She had no way of knowing the frantic haste with which he had summoned the senior Casualty Registrar, or of the phone call that had woken an eminent immunologist from his sleep. She knew none of this—only that she had seen him climb from Claudia's car at five-forty in the morning.

She was naïve, she supposed, for she knew very well that most doctors played the field. Yet she had thought Philip was different. With a terrible kind of sadness she realised he wasn't. But how could a man have held her, kissed her the way he had, and not felt something so deep, something . . .

Oh, forget it, she would think the next minute. She had simply been alone and available in his flat late at night. And she hadn't exactly pushed him away—now had she? What man wouldn't try it on? A genuine case of mistaking lust for love. She tried a brave little laugh and it failed miserably.

Maggie gave up. She couldn't get her thoughts straight and she was as confused and sick at heart as when she started. So that when Alec Blakelock rang up to ask if he might take her to Tom Gibson's party, though she nearly fell over in surprise, Maggie said yes. When in Rome . . . she thought, putting the receiver back. Doubtless Philip would be there with Claudia; it wouldn't hurt half as much if she was on another man's arm. And Alec wasn't so bad. His jokes were dreadful, but at least he was tall and very good-looking.

Her mind made up, albeit with gritted teeth, Maggie walked back up the stairs to think about what she should wear. Sitting down on her bed, she had to admit to feeling a little strange: they had told her in Cas that she might have a mild reaction to the injections. There had certainly been enough of them, even a mild analgesic. 'Give you a good sleep,' the doctor had said.

To be honest, she didn't really feel like going out, and especially not to a party. On the other hand, she didn't want to sit at home staring into space and jumping like a scalded cat each time the phone rang. Who knows, a couple of drinks and she might even enjoy herself.

But what to wear? She wished Jane were home, but she had left early. Maggie opened her wardrobe door and her eyes fell on the lurex dress that Liv had designed. She had never worn it, and had never thought to. But now she took it out of the cupboard with a pensive look.

Philip wouldn't like her wearing it, was her very first thought. Her hand dropped limply, and the glimmering material crumpled on the floor; what on earth did it matter, she asked herself angrily, what he thought? She didn't want his approval, she'd wear the thing and be damned!

She didn't care—she didn't. The thought stayed with her as a lump in her throat, even as she saw how beautiful the dress was on. She walked a circle, her hands on her hips, twisting her head to see the long liquid droop that showed off the graceful line of her back.

Then she realised the whole effect was spoilt by the coarse crêpe bandage on her arm. Somewhere at the back of her mind she remembered an old pair of black lace gloves that had been her aunt's. Rummaging around in her drawers, she found them at last and pulled them out for a critical inspection. On, she found they added just the right note of sophistication.

The night was warm. Not bothering with stockings, Maggie slipped her feet into black suede high heels, then brushed her hair into a pile of curls on top, securing them with a diamanté comb. The effect was stunning.

Alec Blakelock nearly tripped over their front step as he arrived and saw her coolly poised at the open door. He had never really fancied girls with flaming red hair —their skin either burned or freckled, and he wasn't keen on either. He could imagine Maggie had been one of those skinny little kids, all knees and eyes and fat pigtails, and a sea of freckles.

But this ravishing creature? He couldn't keep his eyes off her as she poured him a drink. Maggie sipped hers demurely, while he talked with what he hoped was his usual charm and wit; Alec wasn't a modest man. The phone rang as they were leaving and he paused on the steps outside, but Maggie seemed not to hear it. She walked steadily past him and stood waiting by the car. Her indifference, the sheer untouchable quality about her intrigued him; with a shrug, he left the phone to ring and followed her down.

Philip dropped the receiver back on its cradle and stood staring blackly into space. Either everybody in the house was out and Maggie sound asleep . . . Or had she herself gone to the party? And the devil if she had. He had impressed upon her the foolhardiness of doing such a thing. The stab wound had been nasty, for all that it hadn't penetrated very deeply, and the injections she'd had could knock her for six.

He poured himself a good stiff drink and tossed it down, then irritably paced up and down his living-room floor. Heaven only knew, the day had been bad enough without worrying himself now over Maggie. Though why the hell should he?

The police had to do their job, like anyone else, but the inquiry had consumed an intolerable amount of his time. And then Claudia had made a scene at having to do Maggie's duty. About time she did a turn at late shift. But God, what a mood she had been in!

Philip wished now he hadn't got her the upstairs flat. It was too close for comfort. He had done it as a favour, because they had remained friends over the years—and that was the way he wanted to keep it. When he had arranged for her to have the use of the flat, Claudia had been engrossed in an affair and he had thought himself quite safe from her attentions. But from the state she was in when she turned up this morning, he reckoned that the relationship had soured.

Though it was lucky for him she had come back in her car when she did, and was able to give him a lift to the hospital. He directed a few unspeakable thoughts at the cretin who had slashed his tyres, leaving him without transport—a fate that had also befallen several of his neighbours.

He went to refill his glass, and as he nursed it, his thoughts returned to Maggie. He hoped she hadn't gone to that party. Damn it! He had decided to give it a miss, planning an early night of it—he needed one. But the thought was useless now, so he closed his eyes. The girl wasn't satisfied with upsetting his life, she had stolen his peace of mind as well.

Even Tim's letters were full of her. Had he seen her? Did he think she would come to his school sports day, would he ask her? Philip sighed. Maybe he would, though he hardly thought Maggie would be interested.

When Philip got to the hotel the party was buzzing. He

made his way between the throngs of people and glass cases full of instruments and surgical devices, searching for the one face he wanted to see.

Maggie was finishing her third glass of champagne, and although laughter came bubbling up without any effort on her part, she was wondering why Alec's jokes seemed even less funny than usual; he had his arm round her waist and he insisted on speaking with an atrocious American accent.

In their group there was a lot of laughter and talk about the way doctors practised in the States, and the ticker tapes they kept in their offices for keeping tabs on the stock market. Only Duncan retained his habitual gloom. 'If I don't go into private medicine,' he sighed, 'I'll have to emigrate to New Zealand. The hospitals there give free accommodation. Kids would be able to play in the garden.' He sighed again. He was so despondent he made them all laugh.

Someone moved and Philip spotted Maggie, glass in hand, laughing face upturned; he felt an undeniable spasm of jealousy when he saw it was Blakelock. Then he took in the dress, the slashed front, the curve of breast plainly visible—and when she turned, the sharp exciting incurve of the small of her back. Out of the corner of his eyes he saw Tom Gibson making in his direction. Ignoring his advance, Philip pushed himself through the crowd, gaining Maggie's side in several long strides.

Maggie gave a tiny gasp as Philip's fingers closed on her upper arm in a steely grip; she was detached from the circle of Alec's arm in one smooth movement. He glared over her head at Alec. 'She's in no condition to be here!' he snapped. Fortunately there had been a drift away and the three had become separated.

'Oh, I say, old man!' blustered Alec, seemingly for once at a loss for words. 'Well, I say, it was only a scratch, she's fine now.' Recovering, he grinned disarmingly. 'As you can see.'

Philip's look had narrowed ominously. 'I'm taking her home.' His glance dropped to Maggie, his professional eye automatically registering how much the effort was costing her; Maggie wanted to snatch her arm back and tell him she had no intention of going home—and certainly not with him. But the truth was, she was beginning to feel far from well. His steadying presence was a relief, though she hated herself for being weak enough to need it. Trust Alec, she thought, to just stand by and let Philip bully him!

And then Philip was steering her across the room, adroitly avoiding several attempts to buttonhole them by people wishing to speak to either of them. Outside, Maggie struggled to free her arm from the hard grip. 'How dare you come stamping in there, ordering me about . . .'

He gave a short mirthless laugh. 'I haven't started ordering you about yet, young lady!' but he released her. 'I thought I told you to lie low after those injections,' he growled. 'God damn it, Maggie, you should know better than to mix alcohol,' adding for good measure, 'You drink too much anyway.'

Maggie's mouth dropped open. Nothing could be farther from the truth, it was ludicrous and not worth the trouble of denying. Instead she couldn't resist turning the comment to her own advantage and unleashing a shot of her own.

'I drink too much?' She laughed. 'And my word, you were quick to take advantage of it the other night!' Philip scowled at this veiled reference to their kiss and yanked open the door of his car for her to get in.

In a defiant mood, Maggie pulled a packet of cigarettes and a lighter from her purse; no smoker herself, she had been merely keeping them for Alec. Philip, dropping heavily into his seat beside her, took the packet from her grasp and flung it out the window. 'You can quit smoking as well,' he grated.

Maggie thought of all the unpleasant things she would like to do to him, but she felt too awful to care enough even to protest. Arrogant beast!

'No one at home,' she commented, as Philip pushed open the door on a quiet house.

He looked round and said grimly, 'I wouldn't expect anyone to be home yet in this household, it's too early.' Ignoring his comment, Maggie fumbled for the light switch. The light caught her defenceless. She looked white and exhausted and vulnerable. She drifted rather than walked to the stairway.

'Thank you for seeing me home,' she said, turning. 'I'm sorry,' a desperate note had crept into her voice, 'you'll have to see yourself out.' Philip stood by the front door, acutely aware of her and troubled. He looked over at her, then silently he stepped forward and picked her up as though she were a child.

He carried her up the stairs and through to her bedroom, placing her gently down on the bed. Leaning over her, he looked into the grave dark eyes. Her skin was flushed and sweet, and he reached out a hand and stroked her hair back. Maggie rolled her head, trembling, and he remembered the warm, urgent, desirable feel of her, and his blind impulse was to take her back into his arms and kiss her.

With an effort he straightened and rammed his hands into his pockets. 'Maggie,' his voice was husky, 'listen to me—I want you to get straight into bed when I leave, understand? No waiting up for the others. You're not as strong as you think.' He hovered by her bed, torn by his desire to stay—there was no one in the house either. He felt himself going hot. While he still could, he walked to the door.

All Maggie wanted was to have him come back. She wanted to feel his fingers tenderly smoothing her hair back from her hot face, she wanted him to tell her Claudia meant nothing to him.

'Philip . . .' She called his name, then her stubborn pride dried up her voice and made her throat ache with the effort of holding back all the things she wanted to say.

At the doorway, Philip stood motionless. If he went back and kissed her now, in this tender mood, there was no telling where it would stop. He drew in a long breath. If she reached out her arms for him, he could not have prevented himself from going to her.

When she didn't, he asked, in a voice unintentionally gruff, 'Well, what is it?' Standing in the shaft of hall light, his body poised and tense, he looked angry, and Maggie bit her lip and turned her head away.

'It doesn't matter,' she said dully. She stared at the wall, waiting. For what? For him to tell her that he hadn't kissed her that night in a careless moment? That it meant something to him? That he hadn't spent the night with Claudia?

Philip thrust his hands back into his pockets and clenched his jaw. He ached to have her arms reaching for him, her soft mouth open. His voice choked and tight with emotion, he said at last, 'Are you asking me to stay with you . . . Is that it?' His voice sounded curiously indifferent.

Maggie thought she read contempt in his voice. Did he think she was inviting him to spend the night with her? The icy realisation made her own sound as brittle as glass. 'No,' she said, her coldness driving him away. 'Never . . . I just want you to go.'

The pain she inflicted caught Philip unawares. It was something new to him. His wife had certainly never cut him to the quick, or aroused the same feeling—or whatever it was he felt for Maggie.

This morning when she had looked at him, her blue-grey eyes were rounded and somehow grieving. He had known something was wrong. But there hadn't been time then to find out—besides, the business with the car had upset him and he had been moody and depressed himself. Then this appalling attack . . . Well, one thing, it had certainly stirred hospital security up. He had also found out how important Maggie was to him.

His breathing was ragged. 'If that's what you really want . . .' He waited, hoping, but her face was still rigidly set to the wall. He turned abruptly, his feet punching the stairs on his way down. Maggie let out her breath in a dry sob. She listened for the front door, and heard it slam shut with a finality that made her wince.

CHAPTER EIGHT

THE RINGING of the phone half woke her. Maggie extended a hand from the tangled sheets, groping for it, thinking she was at the hospital. It stopped and she thankfully dropped back to sleep.

Then Nigel was calling her, and she sat up staring at her clock, blinking in surprise because it was only seven in the morning and she was supposed to have the day off. 'Maggie!' Nigel knocked on her door, and she pulled on her robe, flinching at a surprisingly sharp pain that shot up her arm.

It took a full few seconds to recognise the voice on the other end of the line, and when she did her brow furrowed with perplexity. 'John! Why are you ringing at this hour? Something must be the matter . . .'

'Maggie—now take it easy. Your dad's in hospital, and I thought you might want to get the early train up here.' Maggie clenched the receiver and listened in shocked disbelief. 'A coronary, Maggie. But he's all right—well, you know . . . It's a fairly mild one, they say. He's in the coronary care unit at the York Royal. Actually, I'm ringing from there. I've talked to him, he says to tell you he's fine.'

Just like her father to think of her. Maggie clung to the phone like a drowning man to a raft on a lonely sea; all the years he had been there for her, whenever she needed him. It was unthinkable . . . 'I'll be up on the very next train,' she said quickly. Without thinking she put the phone back and flew up the stairs to get ready.

She was halfway to the station before she realised she had hung up on John without a word to him personally. She hadn't even asked him what he was doing in York, though she expected he had gone home for a few days. Even so, her thoughts didn't remain long with him. She kept picturing her father in a hospital bed, ECG wires taped to his chest. She visualised the screen where the pattern of his heartbeat would be recorded. In her worst moments she imagined the ping, and then the ink running in that one long terrible line.

John was waiting for her when she arrived tightlipped and shaken at the station. He took her straight from there to the hospital. Maggie had prepared herself, but her father's thin, tired face came as a crushing blow to her. His eyes, still a vivid blue, had never looked old before, as they did now. But he had a wry smile for her.

Not trusting herself to speak, Maggie stooped to kiss him, then groped blindly for a chair. 'Now don't you fret, lass—the doctor says this is a warning. I'm lucky. A few days' rest and I'll be good as new.'

Maggie tried to swallow the lump in her throat. He was putting on a brave face and she knew that he knew it. She dashed away a tear with an impatient hand; he hated to see her cry. 'Well, you be sure and see you have it, then. No getting on the phone. I hope they've disconnected all the ones round here within reach of you.' She peered at the screen by his bed. 'You haven't got one of your computers installed already, have you?' she asked, joking of course, but not going to be at all surprised to find him hooked up to an operations room somewhere.

'Get away with you!' he chuckled, and although it was a ghost of his old laugh, Maggie was very relieved to hear it. 'John's been . . .' he paused, 'wonderful,' he said finally. He had been going to say, like a son, Maggie thought with a sudden pang. 'He's a good man, Maggie.'

'Yes—I know,' she said painfully. And she did. How much easier it would be if John had been some kind of louse. 'Well . . .' she went on, trying to brighten him with gentle banter, 'look at me, I've come all this way and haven't brought you so much as a grape.'

Her father laughed, his eyes going over her head to someone behind. 'I may not be needing much, from the look of things, lass.' Maggie turned her head to see a young woman standing hesitantly in the doorway, as if undecided as to whether she should come on in or go back out. Her puffy dark brown hairdo pointed up the smallness of her pale, bright-lipped face. She was rather too plump for the splashy outfit she had on, and Maggie wondered if it was this that made her appear rather nervous.

'Come in, darling,' her father said, 'I want you to meet my daughter Maggie.'

This was Moira? Maggie knew a stinging sense of disappointment. She had expected someone quite different somehow, not this woman with her brittle salon prettiness. Moira came forward, her movements jerky.

'Hello,' she said to Maggie. Her small voice was husky. 'I've so much wanted to meet you.'

'Me too,' Maggie was forced to reply, and she hated herself for the high false note in her voice. Nor were they the words she had planned and rehearsed so carefully. To hide her confusion she hurried to draw up another chair. She knew she couldn't fool her father, whose shrewd eyes noticed everything.

Moira's smile was excruciatingly anxious as she placed a heap of brown paper bags on the locker and took a tentative seat on the chair. Filled with remorse, Maggie realised that she was just as much on tenterhooks as she herself was.

As she said, much later, to John, 'I suppose it's because she isn't how I expected her to be. I don't know . . .' In her mind, she saw her mother's soft natural face in the photo she had treasured all these years. John blundered into her thoughts.

They were sitting at home, and, desperately tired, Maggie would have much preferred her own company, but John had insisted on staying awhile. Seeing her father in the CCU had hit her badly, though the worst thing had been the feeling of helplessness at being able to do so little for him. She had only been slightly reassured by the young hospital Registrar, whose grey face and tired manner had seemed enough to make him a likely candidate for a hospital bed himself.

'Maggie, you're miles away! You haven't heard a word I've been saying.' John settled even more comfortably on the sofa and said sententiously, 'In the light of what's happened, we should forget about our little tiff.'

Maggie stared at him. How pompous he is she thought.

'It wasn't a tiff, John,' she said tiredly. It was difficult to remember a time when she had loved him. If she had, it must have been a poor pallid emotion compared to what she felt for Philip. That love, she knew now, was the kind that set a man and woman on fire, then endured with a steady flame that nothing and nobody could put out. She knew it now, and whether Philip reciprocated or not, she would always know it.

John was huffy. 'Well, call it anything you like, but your father would like to see us together again.' At the warning expression on Maggie's face he changed tack. 'At least come on back and work up here.' He nodded at the bandage on her wrist. 'And if you must stay in the nursing profession, you'd find it a lot safer here than where you are at present.'

'I had thought of coming back,' Maggie said quietly, 'and I still may, but right now, I just don't know.'

John said slowly, 'Then you did break our engagement because there was somebody else. It's something I've thought about a lot.'

'I suppose, partly,' she admitted after a moment's pause. 'Though at the time I couldn't know that I loved him—as I do now.' On the verge of tears, she sighed, 'Oh, John, I love him so much!' Her eyes became distant, as though she were staring at some dreadful prospect, and she shook her head slowly. 'But he doesn't love me.'

'Not love you?' John looked quite shocked. 'He couldn't possibly not love you, Maggie.' He had said it in an embarrassed sort of way, and Maggie stared in surprise.

'Why, John, that's the sweetest thing you've ever said to me!' But then the smile faded and her eyes drifted away again. 'He has someone else, you see, and she's really more his type. Oh, perhaps once I thought . . . But he's older than me and been married before, and he has a little boy—and I seem to have gone and given him the impression that I'm not mature enough or something. As if that wasn't bad enough, he seems to think I'm addicted to a round of parties.' John's sandy brows shot up in surprise.

'How on earth did you manage that?' and she giggled weakly.

'I don't know. Oh, I suppose, living where I do—you know Nigel. It was a chapter of misunderstandings, and stupidly I never tried to clear them up. Well, I wasn't really aware of what he must be thinking in the first place—and besides, then, I thought I hated him.'

It proved a relief to talk—it was funny in a way too, because John was the last person she had thought she would ever confide in. 'He's been hurt too,' she said softly. 'His wife was pretty fast on her feet, so I understand, and I expect he's a bit wary. But I'm not like he thinks, and it's all my stupid fault. I go out of my way to antagonise him. The way he treats me, though,' she mused, as if to herself, 'as if I'm a child, and a spoilt one at that.'

So that was it, John thought. He had known from the loss of her old vitality that something was wrong. Something beyond her natural worry for her father—or that psychopath who had attacked her. He shook his head. He had known something like that was bound to happen sooner or later. It was one of the reasons he had wanted her out of the job. Lord, you only had to go into Casualty of a Saturday night! He sighed heavily. Maggie still meant a lot to him, and he hated to see her unhappy.

'You think maybe this other bird has him hooked?' he asked.

Maggie couldn't help but smile. Trust a Yorkshireman to get straight to the point! Her hands gripped one another. 'I think so,' she said. 'At least, I think he spends some nights with her. Though he's at the hospital half the time, so it can't be many.' A smile glimmered briefly and then was gone.

'So you think he's carrying on with her, and he thinks you run round with a fast crowd,' snorted John. 'A pretty kettle of fish! Maybe the two of you should get together and find out what goes, because I know you don't go much for parties, but obviously he doesn't. You might even find he's not all that wrapped up with this other bird as you think.' He shrugged, his face gloomy. 'You know, Maggie, perhaps if we'd talked it out more . . . But, well, that's past history, isn't it? Never too late to learn, though, and you know, that darned pride of yours.' He grinned suddenly. 'Why don't you try talking to him?'

Why didn't she? Always his aloofness had kept her tongue-tied and unable to talk—and her damnable pride had done the rest. After John had gone, Maggie sat for a long time thinking. She understood what he had been saying, or thought she did—all the things that common sense should have dictated ages ago. She loved Philip. More than that, she wanted and needed him. And if she wasn't prepared to lower her pride and fight for such a man as she needed and longed for, then she should have married a good kind sensible man like John, who wasn't aloof and unpredictable and arrogant—and wonderful and tender and passionate and exciting.

Maggie went early to the hospital the next day to see her father. She found him in a buoyant mood. 'There you are, lass. Moira will be along soon—she's booked a lunch table for the two of you.'

'Oh!' Maggie swallowed her dismay, 'But I'm due back in London tomorrow.' She had wanted to take immediate leave, so she could be home to look after him when he came out of hospital, but he wouldn't hear of the idea, claiming that he was being treated as a cardiac cripple already, and so she had left it. Really, in fact, there was no need, because Moira would take care of him. He hadn't said as much, but it was what he had meant, Maggie thought.

When Moira appeared, flustered, her face overheated from the hairdryer, Hadley gave her an adoring look and unabashedly kissed her soundly on the mouth. Her colour deepening by the minute, Moira said breathlessly to Maggie, 'We have to hurry—I'm afraid I'm a little late.'

The head waiter looked impassively down his long nose at them. 'The table was reserved for one, madam. It is now one forty-five.' The restaurant was one of the grandest in the city, Maggie knew, and quite the most expensive. 'But surely you kept it?' Moira asked, after a wild look about at the elegant tables, each of them occupied.

He eyed her sternly. 'We only keep a table for half an hour, madam.'

Moira wilted. 'Yes, of course.' She gave Maggie a hopeless glance. As they walked out again she was close to tears. 'I'm sorry, it's all my fault. My hair was such a mess—and I thought I'd have it done, seeing this was supposed to be a special occasion, and then it took so long. I am sorry.'

'We do not accept any excuses here, madam,' Maggie said, in a perfectly flawless imitation of the head waiter. Moira looked at her and then she and Maggie both burst into laughter. 'Oh, come on, Moira, I know just the place, if it's still there. One can never be sure these days, though. You're just as likely to find a car park or something right where your favourite restaurant used to be.' She linked arms with Moira and they passed the liveried doorman and went out into the street.

Afterwards they recounted the story—much to Hadley's amusement. 'I took her to the Hungry Lamb,' Maggie told him. 'Remember, we used to go there a lot.' They were sitting on his bed laughing and talking: it was one of those rare occasions when Maggie saw her father totally relaxed. She was willing to admit now that it had a lot to do with Moira. And there was good news. The doctor had told him he would be home in another week.

The next day she caught the train back, feeling much less fearful for the future. She was returning to London with a kind of happiness even, and a confidence in herself she hadn't known for a long time. Moira and John had both seen her off and she had thought, as she waved goodbye to them, how lucky she was. Moira was a very special person, and Maggie realised that she liked John much better now, as a friend.

There was a glassy sparkle of late sun on the hospital windows when she arrived. The pigeons who roosted on the ledges were as usual scuffling noisily for the most advantageous position before settling for the night. She ran into Jane coming out of the lift. 'I'm going up to see Bronwyn,' Maggie told her. 'Where are you off to?'

'Canteen. The physios are with her for the mo. Come and have a bite to eat with me. How's your dad?' Maggie told her as they walked along the corridor, Jane nodding sympathetically every now and then. The canteen was crowded, but they managed to get a table in a quiet corner by the window. Jane sat down and took the things from her tray, arranging them on the table. 'Well, go on—tell me! What's your stepmother like?'

'She's not my stepmother yet,' Maggie reminded her. 'But to answer your question . . . awful, I hated her,' she said, grinning from ear to ear.

Jane gulped, then narrowed her eyes in suspicion. 'Margaret Bell, you're having me on! You liked her.'

Maggie laughed at her. 'Well, not at first. But yes, I do now. In fact I like her very much. She's very shy underneath it all—like your Tom.'

Jane said worriedly, 'I hope Tom's family will like me—I must remember to act shy.'

'Be yourself, and they'll like you just fine,' Maggie told her. She took a bite of the indifferent ham and cheese sandwich on her plate, then put it down. 'What's been happening here?' She was dying for news about Philip. Two days she had been away; it was a lifetime.

Jane rambled on until at last Maggie couldn't contain herself any longer.

'Tell me, how's Philip?' she asked—then her voice dwindled as she saw him walk in and join the end of the queue. 'Jane . . .' she said slowly, coming to a decision. There was no time to explain, but they had been friends for a long time and Maggie knew Jane would understand. She chose her words with care. '. . . If you're about finished, you might like to drink your coffee in the common room. I saw Pat go through a few minutes ago.'

'You want me to go and have my coffee with Pat

Mudie?' Jane's eyes roved along the food queue and came to rest on Philip's broad back. 'Aha! Yes—well, I haven't seen Pat in a while, maybe I should go and catch up with the news.' She stood up as Philip turned from the cashier's desk looking for a table to sit at. 'Well, Maggie, I must be off now. See you later,' she beamed.

Maggie's face was pink. She wanted to get up and leave with her friend. But she sat on, like a small animal trapped by the glare of a searchlight as Philip's glance swept in her direction, and hovered.

Her heart gave a painful thump. What if he chose not to come and sit with her? She had not thought of that. Nervous tension stiffened her face, and she stared blindly out the window wishing now she had followed Jane. It would serve her right, she thought, if he did ignore her. Oh God, was he not going to come over? She daren't look. Another moment and she would get up and leave.

'May I join you?'

So absurd and delicious was her relief, Maggie felt she might expire, right there at the table amongst the dishes and salt and pepper shakers. Her eyes travelled slowly up, absorbing the rough hairy texture of his jacket and then the smooth, cleanshaven toughness of his skin where the last rays of sun caught his high cheekbones. Her lashes dropped. 'Yes, please do.' She smiled, her face contained as she moved Jane's dishes to one side.

Philip indicated her arm as he sat down. 'No complications?' and Maggie shook her head. 'I was sorry to hear about your father. How is he?'

His voice was kindly and he listened intently to what she had to say; his face showed concern and yet maintained its aloofness, telling her nothing. When she had finished, a small silence developed between them, Maggie nibbling at her sandwich while he sampled his soup.

'About the other night,' she said at last, and Philip raised his dark eyes enquiringly; he's being far too polite, she thought nervously. She cleared her throat.

'It was good of you to have taken the trouble,' she

seized another breath, 'to see I was all right. And ungrateful of me not to realise it at the time.' Talk to him, John had said. She couldn't. Her words were all wrong and sounded wooden—as if she were reading an unrehearsed part for a school play.

'Oh . . .' His blue eyes were smiling, and Maggie thought bleakly, he has every right to look amused. 'You mean, when I dragged you away from Tom's party? Well, I practically regard myself as your GP now. Consider it part of the service.' His mouth curved—with a hint of mockery, Maggie thought, dropping her eyes to the half-eaten sandwich on her plate.

His knee touched hers under the table and she glanced quickly up and into his eyes, then as he brought his other knee alongside in a deliberate movement, and pressed hers between, a thrill of raw sexuality flowed unchecked between them. At a touch, a single touch, she was drowning. Drowning in the blue of Philip's eyes, caught in the spell of a feeling of urgency so intense that all around was utterly dark, only just the two of them in this one bright moment.

Dimly she heard the chink of dishes and the murmur of voices; Philip too, with a sudden wry smile, as if realising for the first time that they were in a crowded room. Gently he let her go, then leaned his elbows on the table, studying her face thoughtfully. It was the same Maggie, but different, something he couldn't define. It puzzled him. 'I missed you. Why is it, do you think, no one else seems able to pass me the instruments exactly the way I want them?' he asked, watching her closely.

She knew a quick stifling sense of disappointment. She had hoped he might have missed *her*, not the highly trained instrument nurse. And then she remembered the secret touch of knees under the table and realised, perhaps for the first time, that he couldn't put his feelings into words, any more than she could. She thought she understood at last. She glanced up, happy. Happier than she could remember being for a long time.

'I'm glad I'm back, then,' and he beamed at her.

Maggie asked him to tell her about Beth Liddell, and he launched into an up-to-the-minute account of Beth's state of health.

'Oh, but you don't know, do you? I sent her up to Sister Ferguson's ward—as you suggested. See, I do take your suggestions,' he added, and he was smiling broadly. 'She's doing quite well, considering. She has the full use of her arm back, and that is something. Walking on crutches . . .' he paused and a frown gathered between the dark brows. 'She's still on heparin, though.' He was worried about the chances of another clot forming around the walls of the injured blood vessels. Heparin thinned the blood and reduced the chance of that happening, so he had to keep Beth on it. Anti-coagulants were an essential part of her treatment.

Maggie could guess what he was thinking and sympathised with him. They talked about the case, and then as Philip finished his soup she said, 'I was wondering . . . if you'd like to come to dinner some time?' The words hung in the air between them.

'At your place?' He sounded incredulous. Maggie's eyes came up meeting his in a steady gaze. 'Yes, why not? You invited me to supper at yours.'

'Excuse me, you don't mind if I join you?'

Claudia Fanslow stood by the table. Maggie's mouth was still open when she was sitting herself down with a salad and a cup of black coffee. 'How's your father, Maggie?'

Maggie replied automatically, 'Fine, thanks.'

'Good. And I can see you're fit and well. When do the sutures come out?'

'Not for another six days,' said Philip, answering for her. Claudia's sigh told Maggie how boring it was of her to go and get an arm injury. For of course, until the wound completely healed Maggie was unable to scrub, and it threw Claudia's roster out. She gave Maggie an appraising look with her cool eyes, then apparently finding her wanting, turned to Philip. 'Are you going to eat all that chicken? No? Well, I shouldn't but it looks so delicious.' So saying, she helped herself freely to a piece. Maggie stiffened. You had to know a person really well to do that.

Damn Claudia, thought Philip, as he saw a shadow cross Maggie's face. 'About that matter we were discussing,' he said, smiling, 'I'd love to come. When?'

'When? Oh!' And then she panicked. She hadn't thought that far ahead. In fact she hadn't given it any thought at all, beyond asking him. She ignored Claudia's quiver of interest and said, 'I'll get back to you, shall I?' then she excused herself and left them with her sunniest smile. Never mind the when and how and what, she thought, her heart singing. He said he would come. More than that, he would love to come.

Bronwyn was knitting something big and blue. 'Pullover for Gary,' she explained, ultra-casual, as if she had knitted him several and this one was only the latest in a long line. Maggie thought the situation sounded hopeful, and as no other information about Gary seemed to be forthcoming, she left it at that. She hugged her own secret to herself—always a wise precaution in hospitals where gossip travels faster than fire—they talked about Bronwyn's progress, which seemed excellent; she was confident of being out of traction in another couple of weeks. Then Maggie told her about the visit home and when that topic was exhausted, asked if she knew Beth was in the ward.

'Beth? Oh, she's in the four-bed room at the end. Harry is with her. Beth has been waiting all day for him to come, she's been hopping around on her crutches. Really nice, isn't it?' Bronwyn sighed and stared into space, then went back to her knitting. Maggie wasn't sure that she meant it was nice Beth was up and about, or nice that Harry was coming to see her, and she didn't have a chance to find out before a delegation of first-year nursing students appeared with earnest faces and a trolley full of wash bowls and towels and a Sister Tutor in tow.

Harry was still closeted with Beth behind the curtains, so Maggie decided to postpone her visit to another time. At home there was a note from Tom Gibson, inviting her to share a meal with Jane and himself that evening. Maggie was delighted, and feeling pleased, she took a leisurely bath and dressed in a simple white linen frock. She was ready when Jane came hurrying in, looking as they all did after hours on duty under bright artificial lights—pasty-faced and hair flattened into greasy rats' tails by the ubiquitous caps. Half an hour later she emerged to answer Tom's bell, sparkly-eyed and face flushed and with her hair in a smoky cloud round her face. Maggie had never realised before how beautiful Jane could look.

The evening passed pleasantly and Tom proved excellent company. He was a generous man with a quiet, dry sense of humour, and Maggie took a liking to him. He was so painfully in love with Jane, it almost hurt to watch, so that when a suggestion came up that they all take a drive through Regent's Park before going home, Maggie declined, claiming that she had to get back and see to her unpacking as she was starting back at the hospital the next morning.

The night was warm and sultry, and she decided to walk the few blocks back to the house: she waved them goodbye, and set off. There was a pleasant stirring in the air and people lingered over their coffee and dessert at the little pavement tables, and on the benches in the garden squares. Dogs walked their owners, glad to be out. It was the sort of evening it was good to be alive in.

A few spots of rain gave the first warning of a downpour, and Maggie quickened her pace. By the time she turned into her street the rain was pelting down. It seemed pointless to hurry now when she was wet through; Maggie rather liked walking in the rain so long as it was warm and pleasant.

And then a figure detached himself from a car and crossed the road some yards behind her. Maggie, only half aware of him, instinctively quickened her step and clutched her bag a little tighter. The street was quiet and dimly lit—ordinarily she would not have given it a second thought, but in the back of her mind lingered a lasting memory of her recent encounter. At the front door she scrabbled in her bag for the key.

'Maggie!'

'Oh!' She put a hand over her heart and wheeled round. 'Philip, it's you—oh, thank goodness! Heavens, I must be getting nervous!'

'So you should—I could have been anybody. Here, let's have the key or I'll be soaked to the skin as well.' Deftly he sorted out the right one and unlocked the door, ushering her in ahead of him.

'You look like a poor drowned rat,' he told her. Maggie was laughing because she had caught sight of herself in the hall mirror. Tendrils of hair streamed into her eyes and her dress was plastered to her body. 'Don't be unkind!' she called after him as he disappeared into the small downstairs bathroom. He reappeared with a towel.

'Not really—I had a very nice rat once. His name was Napoleon, and I let him swim in my bath sometimes. My mother never knew about it, or so she says.' Philip had draped the towel over her head and was gently rubbing her hair. 'That's better. Now you'd better go and get out of those wet things.'

'You're wet as well,' Maggie reminded him; Philip shook his head.

'I'll dry. Now off you go. You'll catch a cold if you stand about in that wet dress,' he warned.

'There you are!' declared Maggie. 'You treat me like a child—you always do.'

With her hair rubbed into tiny curls and her scrubbed face pink and glowing, and the bedraggled dress, how could she look anything but a child? Philip tried his level best to keep a straight face. 'Very well then, how should I treat you?'

'Like a woman,' Maggie said softly, looking up at him from beneath her long lashes.

'A woman,' he said, with gentle banter, his eyes teasing her. As if he wasn't working overtime to keep from noticing the gradual, lovely flare of her breasts beneath the clinging fabric. Maggie shivered suddenly and he raised an eyebrow.

With a wry grin she said, 'Well, I think I'll just go and get out of these wet things.' As if the idea was original, she paused on the stairs. 'Need one of Nigel's shirts or anything?'

Philip said he would be bone dry by the time she got back, and watched the graceful line of her legs disappear up the stairs. He stood there a moment after she had gone.

Maggie stripped off her dress and bra, then pulled on her jeans and a T-shirt and ran back down. Philip was on the sofa, leaning slightly forward with his elbows on his knees; now that he was serious, she could see he was subdued and worried.

'Did you see Beth this evening when you went up to the ward?' he asked, and she shook her head and told him about Harry being there. 'I was hoping you'd seen her, you might have been able to supply a clue.' His voice was drained. 'She's gone,' he said flatly.

'Gone?' Maggie echoed stupidly. 'You mean signed herself out?'

He shook his head. 'No, not even that. She walked out without a word to anyone. I suspect she had it planned. We have no address, nothing.'

There was anger and frustration in his eyes. Maggie went and sat with him on the sofa. For a moment they were occupied with their own thoughts. Then tentatively she reached out and touched his wrist, and Philip laid his strong warm hand over her own.

'Don't be angry with her,' Maggie pleaded. 'Beth was terrified she might have to go back to theatre again.' His thumb caressed her hand, slowly, gently.

'You have it wrong,' he said quietly. 'I'm angry at myself. You see, I saw Beth last night.'

'Tell me about it,' Maggie invited softly when he lapsed into silence, and Philip, tired and worried, explained what had happened.

'When I went up to see her I thought she seemed over-excited. She was talking about throwing away her

crutches and she said she didn't want to take any more medicine. I explained why she had to stay on the heparin. I also tried to prepare her for what might happen should she get another clot in her leg, but she didn't want to know. The very thought put her into a panic. I could see I wasn't getting anywhere, so I left it.'
He paused. Maggie sat silent, aware of nothing but his words and the warm hand pressing hers tightly.

'Beth told me she was getting married, and I said that was wonderful . . . But I could see that unless she walked out of there on her own two legs, it wasn't going to be wonderful. I think she and Harry have gone, with the idea of getting married straight away. And Maggie, if we don't find her, she hasn't a chance. At this point, without heparin, she's a more than likely candidate for another clot. If she'd stayed in hospital she would have had a fifty-fifty chance of keeping that leg.'

'Then we'll have to find her,' Maggie said quietly. 'There must be some address in her records that will put us in touch with her, or the name of a person who could give us a lead. I suppose you've checked with her parents?'

Philip had, and it seemed Beth's parents knew less and cared little what happened to their daughter. 'They came once,' he said in disgust, and a look in his eyes Maggie would never forget. 'Once, when she was coming out of the anaesthetic. They stood and looked at her and then they left.'

Maggie fell into a shocked silence. She found it incomprehensible that parents could be so uncaring about a child of their own. It made it all the more important for them to try and find her. There was something at the back of her mind—a day when she had gone to see Beth in the unit when Harry was there. Then she remembered.

'Harry's mother's address,' she said. 'One of the nurses took it for reference. It's written down in the unit diary.'

Philip turned to look at Maggie—he could have

hugged her. For days he had been depressed and moody, wanting her and yet forcing himself to forget her, because of some stupid notion that she was too young or whatever, and too unsettled to know her own mind. And here she was, with that calm level head of hers that always took him by surprise.

As so often he was wont to do, he cordoned off his thoughts about her with a laconic gesture, raising a provocatively teasing brow. 'If the unit have such an address tucked away somewhere, then what are we waiting for?'

The address Harry had given took them to a decaying street in South-East London; Philip brought the car to a standstill opposite a tatty-looking launderette which corresponded to the number they had noted down. 'He must live above it. I wonder which slumlord owns this little piece of hell?' He added, 'You stay in the car. I'll go up.'

Maggie was already climbing out. 'You should have seen the area I did my midwifery in, and I was on a bike!' Philip grinned at her cheerful optimism and followed her into a foetid hallway and up a flight of stairs, just narrowly missing treading on someone bedded down for the night with a bottle of wine. Maggie was on the landing, peering at a printed sticker tacked to the only door.

'French lessons,' she read. She looked at him and he gave her a wink. 'That might account for the rosy glow,' he said, nodding at the single naked red bulb in the ceiling. He put his thumb on the bell.

The door was opened by a frowzy woman in wrapper and slippers. She stared at them impassively from gin-sodden eyes. 'Yeah?'

With his usual grave courtesy, Philip asked if Harry was at home. She gave him a malevolent look. 'You a copper?'

Philip assured her he wasn't. He told her as much as he thought he had to, in order to get some information out of her, while at the back of his mind he worried that he had brought Maggie to this place. If anything happened to her, if she was hurt in some way, he would never forgive himself.

'I'm a nursing Sister,' said Maggie, offering her most reassuring smile. 'We think Harry might be able to help us contact this patient we're looking for . . . If you could help,' she appealed winningly. The woman folded her arms and prepared to co-operate to the fullest.

'Harry ain't been here all week. An' I've been like a mother to that boy, but he doesn't care about that, does he? No, not him. Treats this place as if it was some kind of hotel . . .' In the course of her tirade Philip managed to elicit two more addresses where Harry might conceivably be located, and they made their departure. 'And you can tell him from me he'd better get back here with the rent money, or else!' the woman yelled down the stairs after them.

'If that's Harry's surrogate mum,' Philip commented, once they were back in the car, 'Beth needs more help than I thought! Let's have a look.' He thumbed through a directory and pinpointed a street, then gave the book to Maggie. 'You'll have to navigate, I'm not all that familiar with that part of London either.'

The address turned out to be a seedy-looking boarding house. Harry wasn't there, and a young girl with pink hair told them sullenly she never wanted to see him neither. The next stop was in Camden Town, and they drew a blank there as well. Philip gave a cursory glance at his watch. 'Nearly two,' he muttered. 'We haven't had much success. I wonder what the chances are of her coming back to the hospital on her own volition? Not much, I suppose,' he said wearily.

Maggie watched his face and worried for him. As much as she was concerned for Beth, she could see the reality of the situation more clearly than he could at that moment. And reality simply meant that Philip had a dozen or more patients he had to see that day; he could not afford to exhaust himself on this one patient.

'I can hardly put out a Missing Persons on her,' he was saying. 'We don't even know if she'd agree to come back for more treatment. There's someone I know on the

police force who might help with a few discreet enquiries, though—and we can try all the register offices.'
Philip turned for home, driving slowly, despite the lateness of the hour.

'I'm sorry we didn't find her,' said Maggie, and he reached his hand over to cover hers, and kept it there.

'So am I. We gave it a good shot, though,' he glanced sideways at her. 'Where were you tonight?'

Maggie told him, though she rather suspected he knew as Tom has probably mentioned it. Philip just needed to talk about matters other than those pertaining to Beth. She started to tell him about home, and her father, and Moira. He listened, interrupting now and then with a question.

As the streets became more familiar she settled into a comfortable silence with him. This area of London she knew and loved. It belonged to the life she led at the hospital, and like so many things now, despite her having known Philip for a relatively short period of time, this part of London was full of him. She watched out for the street he lived in: they would go through it on the way, and as he turned into it, she let out a little sigh, her eyes searching for the house.

It was then Maggie noticed Claudia's car parked right outside. She frowned, refusing to think anything of it, but it wasn't so easy to dismiss as all that. When people worked in a close-knit unit like theatre, their lives became known after a time. But not Claudia's. It occurred to Maggie then that she really didn't know where Claudia lived, what she did, or with whom, for that matter.

She sat for a time, keeping her thoughts to herself, but then she couldn't help it and she said, 'That was Claudia's car outside your front entrance?'

'Was it? I didn't notice,' Philip said lightly. Maggie looked at the hardness of his profile and wondered if he was lying. Or perhaps, she thought, with a cold numb feeling beginning to take hold of her, he hadn't noticed the car because it was always there.

CHAPTER NINE

'IT's after two in the morning,' said Maggie, her eyes seemingly intent on the passing houses. 'A little late to be visiting, isn't it?' There was suddenly a yawning gulf between them, where before had been a companionable silence. The warm reassuring hand that had been lightly touching hers shifted away slightly, and Maggie felt a chill cramp her stomach. 'Is she living with you?' she asked, her voice painfully low.

'Good lord—the entire hospital would know about it if she were!' Philip's laugh was light. 'Whatever gave you that idea anyway?' Maggie's hands were so tightly clenched her fingernails bit into her palms.

'Oh, the other morning, I suppose—when I saw you get out of her car at around five-thirty,' she replied, determindly casual.

'Ah,' he said, 'so that's why you were on your high horse! You know, I wondered . . .' His hand felt for hers and when she jerked it away, he shot her a brief look. 'You're not going to believe this, but she turned up just as I was about to go and call a cab . . .'

Maggie cut in.

'At five in the morning? She just happened to turn up?' How gullible did he think she was? Her eyes stung as she said sharply, 'That was convenient for you.'

Philip cocked another sideways look; she was sitting as far away from him as it was possible for someone to sit in the front seat of a car.

'Here,' he said, 'I do believe you're jealous, Maggie Bell!' He was grinning hugely.

Jealous . . . Oh yes, he would enjoy that. Maggie could just imagine him going back to Claudia, and the two of them laughing over it. 'This will do nicely,' she said coldly. 'Please drop me here.' Philip's fingers bit into her arm.

'Now wait . . .' He drew the car into the kerb. Though Maggie had been staring out the window for the past five minutes, she had no idea which street they were in. Philip cut the motor, then turned her to face him, a hand cupping her chin and forcing it round.

'You little idiot! Look at me,' he snarled softly, as she jerked her head back again. 'Surely you've known Claudia has the small attic flat above mine? It isn't that much of a secret, for crying out loud. Or I certainly never meant it to be. The truth of the matter is she spends most of her free time at her boyfriend's flat. The other night they had a row, or so I gather, and she packed her things and left. A funny time to do it, I admit, but that's love for you.'

'Oh!' Suddenly Maggie felt very foolish. 'It was just that I thought—well, I thought . . . And then when she picked that piece of chicken from your plate, it was such a familiar thing to do. I . . .'

Philip pulled her roughly to him and began to kiss her face.

'You goose, I've known Claudia for years,' he mumbled, and kissed her again, moving his body against her, his mouth going slack as the contact stiffened him with its unbearable sweet, yearning pain.

'Philip . . .' Maggie's voice held an unsteady note; she was as aroused as he. His lips brushed down the side of her throat, obliterating every single thought from her mind, while his hands caressed and teased until she was moaning, her body arching against him. Neither noticed the car pull in ahead of them, and they broke apart as the door slammed shut.

Maggie looked at Nigel in confusion and then realised they were only a little way from their own front door. 'I'd better go in,' she breathed. 'You don't think he saw me, do you?'

'He wasn't looking particularly,' said Philip with a black look in the direction Nigel had taken. 'And what am I supposed to think about your living arrangements?' he growled.

'Oh, Philip,' Maggie giggled, 'if you knew him you

wouldn't even have to ask! He's a real sweetie. And I don't racket round going to a lot of parties either,' she added.

'How was I to know that?' he said, nuzzling her hair, in no hurry to let her go. Maggie sighed, letting her head rest against his shoulder. There was so much she had to tell him, so much she wanted to ask, but later, not now. Later there would be plenty of time. Wrapped in his arms like this she only wanted to hold on to him and be held, feel his heartbeat, imagine how it must feel to wake up in his arms each morning with the full length of his warm strong body beside her, his lips in her hair. 'You know you're on duty again in a few hours . . .' he said, and she nodded, not caring. 'And that you're running the minor ops theatre for me and that I'm not going to give you a moment to call your own.' Laughing a little, Maggie reluctantly withdrew from the comfort of his broad chest. At the door he tilted her face up, kissing her nose playfully and then a long sweet kiss on the lips.

'We do a very good mug of cocoa,' she said, when he had drawn away, and he laughed down at her.

'Don't make it any more difficult for me to leave you than it already is,' he pleaded.

At last he wrenched himself away, before desire forced him to find her mouth again—and he forgot the hour, and the fact that he was behaving like a boy seeing his first girl home. When Maggie was safely in, he ran lightly down the steps, humming some half-forgotten tune. He got into his car and pulled away smiling.

One day each week Philip operated in the minor Ops theatre—small cases that required a local anaesthetic only. Patients were given a day bed in the adjacent recovery room and went home that night. It was usual for Maggie to scrub and assist him in the theatre on those days, impossible now because of her arm, so she was scheduled to be the one to organise the receiving and the recovery of the patients.

It made a nice change, and Maggie was looking forward to it, because the patients were awake and a cheerful, good-humoured lot on the whole. They would sit up afterwards and enjoy a cup of tea and a chat and swap stories before getting dressed to go home. With some eight cases in the morning, and often another seven in the afternoon, it made for a busy day.

Maggie had been the first to arrive that morning. She should have felt tired, but she wasn't—not in the least. She was ready with a cup of coffee for Philip when he came striding in, freshly shaven and smelling of soap and unbelievably handsome in a classic blue button-down shirt and beige cotton trousers.

He had given her a look of his own, taken in the flawless skin and soft hair springing into wayward curls at the back of her neck where the cap didn't quite cover, and had reached his arms around to push open the door behind her, and with a wicked grin, walked her backwards into the linen closet until she was pressed hard up against the wall.

'Philip . . . someone will come!'

'Kiss me, then,' he had demanded, his blue eyes dancing. Maggie had clenched her arms tight to her sides and shut her eyes, a soft gurgle of laughter in her throat, and they had flown open as she felt the fire in the muscular thighs hard against her.

'Told you,' he laughed. 'Now kiss me, and make it quick, or I won't answer for the consequences.'

She felt his hands edging her flimsy cotton dress upwards over her knees and gulped, 'Philip . . .'

She had kissed him, her blood racing as he forced her mouth open hungrily. Then he was demanding that she take her cap off, laughing down at her, one sexy black brow raised. She put her hands up and held on, shaking her head vehemently and laughing at the same time.

'All right,' he sighed at last, 'I'd better go before I make love to you amongst the sheets and pillowslips. I hope to God there's no one around yet—one look at you, all flushed and tousled, and the secret's out!'

After that, Maggie had caught only a glimpse of him as she escorted the patients into theatre and arrived to take them back to the recovery room. When Alan Bradford came down to do an arm block on a patient, she was busy sorting notes into order. He came over to the desk. 'Full house this morning,' he said, nodding at the row of beds. 'New girl on her feet still?'

The new girl he referred to was Hannah Staz, Sue Manning's replacement and Claudia's latest recruit. With so little experience in theatre work, it seemed to Maggie unnecessarily cruel sending her down to assist in Minor, where she was stuck in with the doctors by herself without anyone to turn to for help. Claudia believed in throwing her nurses in at the deep end; if they survived, they stayed. In Maggie's opinion, a lot of good nurses were lost in this way.

'If Gary has anything to do with it, she'll still be on her feet,' Maggie answered, and felt a twinge of disloyalty as she thought of Bronwyn upstairs doggedly knitting the outsize pullover in her hospital bed.

'Ah,' said Alan, 'being pretty helps, eh? Though it won't get her very far with Philip. Skill counts with him. Lord, is that the time? I'd better get some local into this man with the arm. Got everything set up?' Maggie went with him to the curtained bed at the end, where a thin balding man sat nervously on the edge.

'Mr Sinclair, Dr Bradford is here to put some local anaesthetic in your arm.' Maggie smiled reassuringly and left Alan's wizardry to do the rest. She stood by the patient's side while Alan explained very carefully, exactly what he was going to do. The man nodded thoughtfully. 'Good,' said Alan. 'Now lift up your arm—that's the way . . .' He prodded the axilla with expert fingers.

'Not there, doctor!' Mr Sinclair cried in alarm. 'The lump's on my wrist.'

Alan patiently pulled up a chair and sat down and began his explanation all over again. 'I'm going to inject the local into your armpit, Mr Sinclair, that's all . . .' He explained how that would deaden all the nerves so there would be no pain in his arm. 'It's what we call an arm block.'

'I'd rather just have a prick on my wrist, if you don't mind,' said Mr Sinclair, sweating gently, his hand protectively in his axilla. Alan had already explained at some length that it would take more than an injection in the wrist to deaden the pain of removing a gangloin from the tendon sheath, and for once he found himself stumped. He looked pleadingly at Maggie, but the buzzer had gone, and she had to go and receive the next patient from Theatre.

Hannah was waiting in the corridor outside the theatre with the patient in recovery position on the trolley. Maggie grabbed one end and the two swiftly wheeled him into a bay in the recovery room. Quickly she checked the notes, then leaned over his side. 'Mr Allsop!' she called. The man stirred, but didn't waken.

'We had to give him morphine,' Hannah told her.

'All right, let's take his obs,' said Maggie, and took the stethoscope from around her neck, plugging the metal ends into her ears and linking up the sphygmomanometer with the cuff around his arm. She pumped, then paused, letting the mercury fall very slowly. 'Same as it was when he came in,' she said, taking the stethoscope from her ears. Mr Allsop stirred then and lifted his head.

'Hello, nurse, what about a cup of tea?' Maggie smiled and settled him more comfortably on his side and promised she would bring one.

'He seems OK,' she said to Hannah as they walked back to the desk. 'Just for a moment I wondered . . . but his obs are stable. I'll keep an eye on him.'

'He only had this little thing taken off his back,' Hannah said. She sounded weary, and Maggie asked sympathetically, 'How is it in there?'

'How is it? Oh, I just dropped a sterile pack, flipped a packet of silk on to the floor, cut my fingers opening an ampoule—that's all.'

'In other words,' said Maggie, 'the usual sort of first day.'

Hannah's smile was rueful. 'If Mr Lonsdale had his wish, I'd be shot at dawn,' she said dolefully.

'He's very nice really—once you get to know him,' Maggie assured her with a smile, sorting out the notes and the X-rays for the next patient, and remembering how difficult she had found Philip in the beginning, how cold and distant and autocratic. Then she thought of the warm wonderful man who held her and kissed her, the feeling of exultation she had, just thinking of him, and the perpetual butterflies. And too, of the sudden terrifying crash into despair that could come at any moment and she could do nothing about, until he was beside her and a look, a glance, a curve maybe of his lips, told her everything was all right and the warmth would flow through her again. She was so terribly in love with him, she shivered when she allowed herself to ponder over it because, for sure, she did not really know if it was the same for him. If he loved her as she did him.

Mr Allsop was a good colour and his pulse seemed perfectly normal, so Maggie left him sleeping peacefully and rejoined Alan Bradford and Mr Sinclair. Alan gave her a grin when she appeared. 'Sister Bell will hold your arm up, Mr Sinclair—and I promise the injection isn't going to be any worse in the axilla than you'd find it in your wrist.' Being the expert he was, the procedure was over within minutes, and Alan on his way back to the main theatre where he had the next patient waiting for him and Duncan in a lather to start, no doubt.

Now that the ordeal was over, Mr Sinclair was prepared to be chatty with the lovely young Sister who was tucking him up. But Maggie was in rather too much of a hurry to talk long; she had a good sixth sense, and right now it was urging her to get back to Mr Allsop. She made her patient comfortable, positioning his arm carefully on a pillow and giving him the bell in his other hand, she left with her usual wide smile.

She slipped quietly through the curtains; she knew at once that he was lying too quietly. 'Mr Allsop!' she said, her voice urgent with apprehension. His eyes stared blankly up at her. Scarcely breathing, Maggie felt for his pulse. None. No discernible pulse or heartbeat, eyes fixed and dilated. Her hand was on the buzzer before her mind had even fully absorbed these facts. Three sharp rings which would be heard in Theatre.

Swiftly she turned him flat on his back, whipping out the pillow and extending his head backward; she had already started mouth-to-mouth resuscitation when the others reached her with the crash cart. Grimly they swung into a well rehearsed routine. Within seconds the mask was on, Gary pumping in oxygen via the ambu bag while Philip compressed the sternum and Maggie drew up the adrenalin.

As the seconds became minutes, she worked feverishly with Hannah to prepare drugs and intravenous infusions; they had the defibrillator hooked up with contact leads, and all the while Philip continued to give cardiac massage. He worked aggressively, pressing straight downward on the chest, using his back and shoulders for strength.

Philip and Gary used a ratio of five compressions to one ventilation. As soon as Philip's hands left the chest, Gary bagged in the oxygenated air and the chest rose and flattened, rose and flattened. Hopeless minutes passed. Suddenly there was a swallowing movement and Philip stopped immediately, feeling for a pulse. 'We've got one!' he said, relief in his voice. And then Mr Allsop started breathing spontaneously.

Hannah was looking very pale. She said in a small wavery voice, 'Is he going to be all right?'

Philip's mouth twitched slightly at the corners as he looked over at Maggie. 'Well, Sister Bell, you're the one doing the electrocardiogram, what do you say?'

'Shows a normal reading,' she said, running off a tape and giving it to him. He grunted and looked up as Alan came charging into the room and was followed by the team from the intensive care unit. As they crowded around the bed, Mr Allsop opened his eyes and blinked. 'Nurse said she was getting me a cup of tea,' he said plaintively.

Alan scratched his head. 'That nurse is awfully slow sometimes,' he said, glancing across the bed at Maggie with a huge grin. 'But I think perhaps we'll make you more comfortable in another bed before you have it.'

'Then do I get a cuppa?' Mr Allsop asked, adding in a querulous tone, 'They give you one straight away in

Private. Never have to ask for it.'

'What's he going to say when they start running him through the post resuscitation routine?' Maggie asked, watching as Mr Allsop was wheeled out through the swing doors and fancying she could still hear him going on about his cup of tea. Beside her, Philip shook his head, the corners of his mouth pulled down.

'He'll most probably never know he had a complete cardiac arrest and had one foot in the grave, and he'll complain for years how he wasn't given his cuppa.' He grinned suddenly. 'You should worry! When he gets out of here he'll sue me for bruising his ribs, most likely—I hope to hell I didn't crack any.'

The touch of black humour lessened the grim tension in his face. But like Maggie, he well knew that it could happen again, at any time; for approximately one cardiac arrest occurred in every twelve hundred operations, and from any one of a number of causes. This time they had been lucky.

And now? Philip glanced at the pile of notes waiting on the table. 'Bring along the next patient,' he said quietly. Maggie watched him lift his shoulders back, as if distributing a heavy weight more comfortably, then turn and walk away from them, back along the corridor to the theatre, a proud and lonely figure, and her heart ached for him.

The rest of the day passed without further incident and they worked hard to achieve a smooth flow of patients in and out of the theatre. Maggie made the last pot of tea for the day, then hurried to get finished, writing up the notes, filling in dates and times on appointment cards, speaking to anxious friends and relatives in the waiting room and eventually seeing her last patient safely into a cab at six-thirty.

Back in Recovery to lock up she found Philip lying nonchalantly on one of the trolleys, his long legs propped up on a radiator. The thought that he had waited for her made Maggie glow with pleasure.

'We're closed, love. Come back tomorrow morning,' she told him heartlessly. Philip fired a pillow at her and she darted for the door with every intention of locking him in.

'I'll unmake all your lovely beds,' he threatened.

'You wouldn't . . .' Maggie tried to sound cross, but she could hardly contain her laughter. His raised eyebrow insisted that he would, and not think twice about it, so she waited for him while he collected his legs and stalked over in a good imitation of Clint Eastwood.

'I wouldn't, eh?' He stood menacingly by her side while she coolly locked the doors. By the time she had dropped the keys off at Reception he had assumed a rather more serious air. 'I forgot to tell you, Maggie, I'm having the register offices checked. Probably be our best chance of getting to Beth.'

Maggie was silent. She was thinking it was going to be some wedding present for Beth, but knowing how important it was that they did locate her, if even just to see if she was all right. She felt Philip's hand on her shoulder, and looked up smiling.

'You're not so tired you can't talk to me?' he asked, and she shook her head. Taking a quick look up and down the deserted corridor, he bent down and kissed her lightly. Maggie blushed and he laughed at her teasingly. 'Hey, and what about this dinner you promised me?'

'Just let me know what evening you have free,' she said, full of confidence. They settled on an evening at the end of the week when they were both free, then Philip had to rush off to his evening lectures, and Maggie slipped up to see Bronwyn for a few minutes before going home.

Later, though, when she had time to think about it, her confidence began to wane. She had been imagining a perfect, romantic little dinner for two: candles, flowers, sparkling glass, the tantalising aroma rising from some exotic dish—and just themselves alone, to enjoy it.

Problem number one—she was a terrible cook. The thought even was enough to bring her out in goosebumps. What on earth had possessed her to ask him? Problem number two—she could almost bet on everyone staying in that evening. She would have to make sure Nigel and Jane were out on that particular evening, and that meant persuading them, and then goodness alone knew the teasing she would be in for.

Maggie was still mulling it over in her mind when Moira phoned as promised, with up-to-the-minute news on Hadley's progress. It seemed that the doctor's prognosis had been correct and her father was making a rapid recovery. The news brought a blessed sense of relief to her, as she had been worrying about a relapse. She had seen it happen too often, and proving such a devastating blow to confidence as to make recovery afterwards twice as long.

Moira went on to tell her about Brownie's success in a baking competition and some small items of domestic news. Then Maggie found herself confiding her worries about the dinner she had so blithely offered to make. 'I do so want it to be very special,' she told Moira.

Moira immediately thought it was for John—she liked John—and Maggie had to tell her about Philip, though she managed to convey that he was only a friend, and that he meant absolutely nothing to her. Maggie couldn't let anyone know how important Philip was to her, as if such an admission would be begging for disaster.

If Moira wondered why the dinner had to be so very special for a friend who meant absolutely nothing to Maggie, she refrained from commenting and poured forth a number of suggestions. But Maggie ended up more confused than she was at the beginning. It was Nigel who came to her rescue. She was mooching about, dolefully peering into the cupboards, when he arrived home.

'Hello, darling . . . nice to find you in the kitchen.' It wasn't Maggie's usual haunt. 'Nothing wrong, is there? You look a bit peaky.' Maggie was only too pleased to tell him what was wrong, and they settled down at the table with a fresh pot of tea. She didn't actually ask right out if he would be in that evening, she was hoping he would bring up a suggestion himself. She glanced at him and he seemed to be brooding. 'How's Liv?' she asked, thinking she hadn't seen her for ages.

'Oh, she's fine, actually,' Nigel replied, a shade too quickly. Then he smiled and said with something like his usual gaiety, 'I might ring her up, take her out that night, if you're going to be entertaining.'

Maggie felt guilty, he had looked so sad, and mumbled, 'Oh, you don't have to, Nigel . . .'

He grinned. 'Yes, I know, but I'd like to. Now let's see about your dinner party.' He pulled a pad over and made some jottings. 'Fillet steak, a wine sauce—don't worry, it's easy—jacket potatoes, broccoli maybe, a fresh crisp salad, followed by—oh, one of those French apple tarts. I know the best place where you can get one, and cream of course. Finish off with cheese and crackers—nothing to it. And if you want, start with a small mound of fish pâté, top with cress and serve with triangles of crisp toast.'

'And you say that's easy!' Maggie said dubiously. Nigel was already busily making lists and calculations; he seemed to be enjoying himself hugely.

'Have him arrive eight-thirty at the earliest,' he told her. 'By then you'll have had your bath and a couple of glasses of sherry and be floating about on a cloud of your sexiest perfume. In other words, he won't stand a chance.'

'Nigel . . .' Maggie began, going pink.

'Ah, but good cooking is the way to a man's heart, though. Always was, always will be,' he said, subsiding into gloom. 'I wish Liv knew that. She thinks that because I actually like cooking, I want to do it all the time.' He laughed suddenly. 'You didn't know my burning ambition was to be the chef at a famous restaurant, did you?'

Maggie went to work the next morning feeling on top of the world. She had a list of all the items she needed, the times written down, of what to do when, so that when she came in from work all she had to do was refer to the list and work through it—what could be more foolproof than that? She walked happily into the scrub room and found Duncan muttering to himself.

'You're early,' she said brightly. 'It's not often anyone beats Philip in,' and humming under her breath, she started opening the gowns up.

'I'm always here on time,' said Duncan, looking for an insult and ready as ever to take umbrage. 'But in any case, I'm doing the list today—and tomorrow, as it happens—Philip has gone to Tim's sports day.' Maggie felt a twinge of doubt. She looked at him, startled. It was on the tip of her tongue to say that no, he wouldn't go, not without telling her. Of course she didn't. But she was still standing in the middle of the room like a ninny when Claudia sauntered in looking pleased with herself.

'Sister Bell, I asked Cas to have a look at those sutures on your arm—I'm sure they could come out. A touch of surgical spray and you could scrub and assist Duncan.'

'A bit early yet, isn't it?' Duncan said, but Claudia ignored him.

'Oh, I'm sure not. Sister Bell is young, and young people heal so well.'

Why did she feel that Claudia was referring to something other than her wrist injury? Why the stupid niggle of doubt and suspicion? It was absurd to go looking for hidden messages. Maggie thought, I'm getting as bad as Duncan!

In the canteen at lunchtime, Jane said, 'You didn't say Philip was going away for two days.' She sipped her coffee while Maggie's went cold on the table.

'That's because he didn't tell me,' she said, adding defensively, 'He doesn't tell me every little thing.'

'Oh well, I thought . . . You seem to be pretty friendly these days, so I thought he might have said. Well, maybe he'll call . . .' Jane said in a comforting voice, pushing Maggie to the verge of tears.

'No reason why he should,' she muttered. 'It's not as if we have any kind of understanding . . .'

If that was what she believed, then why was she sitting home in the dark that evening, waiting for the phone to ring? Because she hoped he would. Because his kisses had promised so much, and because she was hopelessly, blindly in love with him.

Sometimes when he didn't know she was watching him, Philip would look up, and those beautiful eyes of his would be so distant and so cool, and she understood then how self-contained he was. The thought returned to plague her now. Could a man like that ever fall in love with her? Wasn't he too self-contained? Oh, Philip, Maggie thought. Oh, Philip!

But oh, the agony of waiting, hoping for the phone to ring and then when it did, picking it up in an agony of suspense, and then the disappointment when it wasn't Philip's voice on the line. How she wished he would call her, if only to say where he was. She thought a little sadly of John's phone calls. Safe, dependable John. A call every night from practically their first meeting. Someone had once said to Maggie how nice it must be to have a man you could rely on implicitly to call at a certain time each evening. She knew now what they meant, and she wondered if a relationship with Philip would always be fearful and apprehensive—and supposed it would, if that was a part of being truly in love.

But still, she thought, if being called sometimes on the phone meant so much to her, she should ask him. Wind her arms around his, and look up and say laughingly, 'Why don't you phone sometimes?' as if she were half joking. And he would bend down and kiss her and joke back and promise he would, if it made her happy.

But when he came striding along the corridor after her, on the day she expected him for dinner, all her intentions fled in her shyness of him. When he was smiling into her eyes it was quite beyond her to say anything at all. 'All set for tonight?' he asked, his hand gently caressing the soft inner part of her upper arm, and Maggie could only nod.

He stood looking down at her, impossibly handsome; Maggie told him what time he was expected. 'All right, eight-thirty it is,' he said. 'I'll be there, as hungry as a horse,' he laughed. 'Or is it hunter and eat a horse?' He squeezed her shoulder—in the busy corridor he could hardly do more, she told herself—and then was gone. Maggie watched his long quick stride and the white coat flapping behind him; he never buttoned it these days, she thought absently. Was it because he had become a little more carefree?

Standing in the doorway at exactly eight-thirty that night, Philip caught his breath. He had grown too accustomed to seeing Maggie clad in baggy hospital gowns, hair severely scraped back under a theatre cap, face pale and exposed under the harsh lighting. But seeing her like this, with her hair in a soft muzzy cloud of curls still damp from her bath, eyes sparkling in a flushed face and blushing as he bent to kiss her, he knew without a doubt that he was in love with her.

'I got a card from Tim yesterday,' she told him, glancing up shyly, nervous of him now that he was here, filling the hallway with his masculine presence and looking quite impossibly elegant in a light grey herringbone tweed suit and with his dark hair brushed smooth. He had dressed as carefully as she. In defence to Nigel's best pink linen tablecloth and napkins, Maggie had chosen a dress in palest shell-pink jersey. It was years old, but it suited her wonderfully well.

'He said he'd sent one. You know I went down to his sports day?' Philip said casually. Maggie said nothing, though her heart shrank a little. Knowing what he did from one day to the next and having him discuss his plans meant so much to her, and so little to him, apparently. He seemed not even to think she might have been interested in knowing about Tim's sports day.

But at dinner she could not have wished for a more amusing companion. They sat at a little round table, Philip poured the wine and had her laughing at a fund of perfectly hilarious stories. He told her what Tim had been up to, and a little about his parents. Maggie knew that they lived within a few miles of Tim's school and that they were able to see him often and had him to stay for weekends and holidays. And also that his mother had never got to like Napoleon, the white rat Philip had allowed to go for daily swims in his bathwater.

Maggie was smiling, her eyes luminous in the candlelight, and Philip could feel himself responding, smiling back at her, the lines of discipline and worry erased from his face. When Maggie retreated to the kitchen he went with her, plucking Nigel's outlandish apron from the peg with a wide smile and putting it on. He insisted on doing the steaks, which were waiting to be cooked, tender and succulent on a plate. The wine sauce produced the kind of aroma Maggie had dreamed about, the jacket potatoes, cooked to perfection, came on cue from the oven, she even remembered a sprinkling of chopped onions for the broccoli.

'When do you expect your father home?' he asked. They were still at the table, lingering over coffee, Philip puffing contentedly on a cigar. He was smiling and at ease.

'Next week, if all goes well. And then I wouldn't put it past him to get married straight away,' Maggie said happily.

'Couldn't think of a better way to convalesce myself,' Philip said with a devilish look in his eye, and Maggie thought it was all turning out so beautifully. Her father would be home, and she knew Moira was going to make him happy; and the evening she had planned for Philip had worked out better than she had dared hope for. She thought blissfully of the extravagant compliments he had paid her. No use worrying yet that he thought she could make better apple pie than his mother!

They stood up from the table in a hushed mood, a bond of understanding between them, a knowledge that they were going to make love. Philip bent and kissed her lips softly. 'Did you have to bribe the entire household to stay away?' he murmured, his mouth against hers.

Maggie tilted her head back, looking up at him. 'Until midnight,' she whispered, her eyes dark as the night. Fingers steady, she slid the knot of his tie loose and unbuttoned the neck, then drew her hands down over his shirt, feeling the hard masculine chest beneath her palms.

The sensuousness of those delicate hands darkened

his senses with desire. He drew her close and found her mouth, kissing her passionately, wanting more and more of her. Her skin was flushed and sweet, her whole body trembling, and in a sudden frenzy he began kissing her shoulders, her throat, her little cries of pleasure driving him on. They clung to each other, Philip covering her face in kisses, as if he had lost and only just found her.

He heard the phone ringing with a kind of hatred. Maggie, totally lost, delirious in his arms, looked up in bewilderment. 'Maybe it's the hospital. I'll have to answer the damned thing.' But he held her for another few precious seconds, rocking her in his arms as if she might not be there for him when he returned. Then reluctantly he let her go. Maggie sat down again and wound her legs around the chair. Even her bones seemed to have turned to buttermilk, she thought, her eyes dreamy. All she could think was that this man was life itself to her.

'The ambulance just brought Beth in.' Philip stood in the doorway, his face grave with concern. 'And by all accounts, her leg is pretty well shot.'

Maggie caught her breath, her dreams fleeing in the face of this stark news. 'Can you do anything?' His eyes rested on her. Already he had changed, become isolated, already she felt the pain of parting.

'I'm going to grab every last chance, but I don't know.' He added grimly, 'I'll find out in a hurry, though.'

CHAPTER TEN

'WHAT THE . . . ?' Philip swore under his breath as the hosing came loose from the foot pump and splattered him with pink antiseptic.

'At least you'll be clean,' Maggie said beside him, in as bright a voice as she could summon. Considering Philip had been up since five that morning with Beth and had spent the intervening hours worrying about her, it wasn't so surprising he was on the short-tempered side. All being equal, he seemed the same highly competent surgeon Maggie had always known, confident, and capable of enduring the long hours of sustained concentration that lay ahead. But then he would turn and she would see a look of shadowed fatigue in his blue eyes that worried her every bit as much as the pinched look of defeat that had settled on Beth's face.

As Maggie rinsed her arms with running water, regretting the healed wrist that made it possible for her to take part in this operation, Pat Mudie came to the door. 'What is it, Pat?' Maggie asked quietly, seeing her hesitate—and as Philip's expression was growing grimmer by the minute, she delivered a look that begged her to get on with it.

'Maggie, Beth's asking to see you again. She says it's important. I told her you were scrubbing and wouldn't be able to . . .' Pat's eyes went nervously to the surgeon. 'But she got hysterical then, and now she's refusing to have the operation at all unless you go and see her.'

Philip knocked the tap off with his elbow and silently began drying his arms. Maggie was well aware she would be holding him up if she went, but making up her mind quickly she addressed herself to Pat. 'If that's the case then of course I must go.'

'We should just get on with it,' said Philip, his voice

gritty. 'Don't for God's sake let's prolong the agony for her. I explained why she had to have this operation, and she seemed to understand—at any rate, she signed the consent form willingly enough.' But he paused, his eyes on the tense little figure in front of him. 'Very well, then,' he said at last. 'Make it quick, though.' His voice expressed a greater latitude than either his words or his dark countenance, and Maggie, with a breath of relief, hurried on her way.

Beth was sobbing, one arm flung over her face. Alan was beside her. He mimed a message to Maggie when she came in and she understood he was unable to go ahead with the induction with Beth in the state she was in.

'Beth dear . . . you wanted to see me?' Maggie asked gently, and the arm was withdrawn, exposing a tear-stained face. Maggie took a tissue and offered it to her with a smile. Beth wiped her cheeks, hiccuping a little as the sobs subsided.

'I won't be put to sleep, unless you promise me they won't take my leg off.' She twisted the tissue in her fingers, her eyes begging.

It was the worst moment in Maggie's life. There was evidence that gas gangrene had already set in, and if Philip didn't go ahead and amputate, he would be condemning Beth to a horrible lingering death.

As she hesitated, the beautiful eyes became distant. 'I'd rather die,' Beth told her. There was a ghastly note of finality in her voice and Maggie knew that everything rested on what she said in the next few moments. She felt Alan's hand on her shoulder and was grateful for the comfort it gave her; it was also a reminder that time was running out. Gas gangrene travelled fast.

'Beth . . .' she swallowed painfully, 'I promise I'll talk with Mr Lonsdale, I promise you that. But that's all I can promise.'

Beth searched her face, and Maggie prayed she would accept what had been said. She had not lied—she would talk to Philip. At last Beth gave a nod. 'All right, I trust you.' Maggie was so shaky when she turned away she thought her legs would never carry her as far as the scrub room.

It was nothing to what she felt when she faced Philip. Once again he appeared to her as the cold aloof surgeon, untouchable, remote. How on earth was she to talk to him? But she had to try—that much she had promised. Philip let her get all the way to the end of her plea, then he said bitterly, 'If she'd come in thirty hours ago, twenty-four even . . . But once gangrene is present in an extremity, no amount of revascularisation will reverse the situation.' Maggie's glass-clear eyes came up to his in the steady gaze he had grown to know and love. Those eyes that made him want to do anything in the world to make them shine with happiness.

Maggie nodded and simply said, 'Yes, I know it. I know also that you'll do all you can and no one else could do better.' She hadn't revealed Beth's last words to her. Let that be her burden. Philip already had an unconscionable one of his own to contend with.

She checked to see that Pat had included his specialised Rongeurs—powerful biting forceps for cutting tissue, particularly bone—while over on the orthopaedic table beside the chisels and hammer lay the bone-cutting saw. Maggie uttered a silent prayer that it would never be needed, and they made a start.

Amputation, in Philip's mind, had always been equated with failure—when he was well aware that the textbooks insisted that a surgeon should view it as an attempt to improve the overall function of the patient. Well, let him, he was thinking, let the author of that particular text come and do the job himself!

The leg was healthy, but the foot was beyond saving—that much soon became obvious. Philip avoided Maggie's eyes, but she knew it as well as he. He straightened his back, hunching his shoulders beneath his gown. Their conversation so far had been monosyllabic and Maggie's eyes had become very dark. No amount of rationalising could ever make what they were doing any the less repellent, that Philip knew well, but he had no option other than to go ahead. In all his life, it was the most dreadful thing he had ever had to do, and he felt a great weariness, not of his body so much, but a weariness of his soul.

Maggie herself went ahead calmly preparing the instruments, although she was torn in two by conflicting loyalties. To Beth who trusted her; to Philip who must do it simply because it had to be done, and someone had to.

As Philip worked, he became more and more withdrawn—deliberately so. For him to give any indication of the emotional stress he was under was unthinkable. He enclosed himself. It was the only way he knew that would enable him to get through the whole messy business. Maggie could see that it was a killing blow for him, and something in her also died a little in that hour.

The next day she stood in Paula Crisp's office, white-faced, hands clenched at her sides. 'I can't bear it—I hate theatre work. Hate it! I wake up at nights sometimes . . .' She stumbled to a stop, thinking of the look on Beth's face when she had gone to see her after the operation.

Paula's shrewd eyes took it all in. Maggie had reached the crisis point. The usual sort of crisis—and Paula had seen many. Nurses got over them, and Maggie would as well. At the moment she was unable to come to terms with her distress, but later, when she saw Beth walking about and enjoying life again, then she would think differently. And Paula knew that with proper postoperative care and a good prosthesis, it was only a question of time before that happened.

Not much passed Paula by, and she suspected Philip Lonsdale had taken it as badly as Maggie had, though it was hard to tell, when the man retreated into himself and walked about with a deadpan face. She sighed. Well, she couldn't order a surgeon off on holiday, but that was what she could order Maggie to do.

Maggie went home and flung herself into the household chores; washing up the usual assortment of dirty dishes left standing on the sink bench and clearing away an accumulation of breakfast things, and banging shut the cupboard doors while she was at it. There was no place for squeamish people in the operating theatre, so why on earth was she thinking of it as a career?

She should at least be able to distance herself emotionally from the person under the green drapes; Philip didn't have that problem, apparently. He managed to distance himself—when it suited him. Or so it looked to Maggie.

Nothing made sense any more—and her chaotic thoughts flew on. Philip was self-contained all right—how much she was only just beginning to find out. And she was glad she had, if he was prepared to ignore his own pain, and hers, and shut himself away behind a blank wall . . . Well, let him. She wasn't like that. She couldn't just anaesthetise herself on cue.

All this came pouring out into Jane's mildly astonished ears. Nurses were notorious for their sudden torrents of pent-up emotions, but it wasn't like Maggie to take her grief and frustration out on someone else, and Philip, of all people! And did she really think she had failed because she had allowed herself to become too involved in a particularly sad case? Theatre nurses were not the unfeeling robots some people thought.

But Maggie didn't really need to be told that. What had really hurt was the way Philip had cut himself off. He was a man who did his suffering alone. Jane could imagine the blow it must have been for him—having carried out a save-the-limb-at-all-costs policy, when other surgeons wouldn't have given it a second chance. As it was, he had performed a miracle in saving the leg itself.

When the impetus had gone from the outburst, and Maggie's face was a shade whiter, Jane thought it time to do something. She took Maggie firmly by her slim shoulders, drew her to a chair, and made her sit down. Then she walked over to the cupboard and brought out a bottle of red wine, glancing at the label before uncorking it.

'Nigel chooses good wine, I'll give him that,' she said, and calmly poured two glasses. 'You do love Philip, don't you?' she asked, as casually as she might ask Maggie if she'd had a good day.

Maggie sat for a long time, very afraid she was going to bawl her eyes out, and she could do without any pitying look from Jane at this point. If she was going to make a fool of herself, she would rather it be in the privacy of her own room. She did, however, permit herself a nod.

Jane by this time had joined her at the table. She pushed over the glass of wine and said, 'If you do love him, then, why not go round and tell him?'

Maggie's fine brows vacillated between a line of doubt and one of open incredulity. 'I thought it was the man who did that sort of thing,' she blurted finally.

'Oh, you are such an innocent!' sighed Jane. It was the kind of voice people used for babes and sucklings. 'The pair of you—honestly! The trouble is, you're too alike. You both hide your feelings too well. And you don't have to look like that, Maggie Bell—you know you do. Every bit the same as Philip. No one must ever know what goes on inside, it's part of your nature, and he's the same way. You say that he's self-contained, but don't you think that he might be thinking the same of you?'

Maggie raised astonished eyes. 'Do you think so?'

Later she climbed the stairs to his flat, half of her wanting to turn and run back while there was still time. But she went on, because she desperately wanted to see Philip, if only to apologise, for she had behaved every bit as selfishly. She saw that now, going off at an emotional tangent of her own. Jane had managed to make detachment sound like the greatest of human virtues, but it didn't prevent her heart beating more wildly as each step took her nearer to his door.

She rehearsed her words carefully, then pressed the door bell and waited with quaking knees. He was at home, that much she knew from the hospital switchboard operator, and a tenant, conveniently going out to walk his dog, had let her in the front entrance, saving her having to talk into the intercom.

She stiffened as the door opened, ready with a lighthearted greeting . . . It froze on her lips as Claudia, not

Philip, stood there. Maggie's eyes took in the pale pink bathrobe and matching towel neatly turbaned round Claudia's head, and all the while she kept denying what she was seeing.

'You look surprised, Maggie.' Claudia's throaty chuckle reverberated in the empty hall, then one stencilled brow rose in query, as Maggie continued to stare with huge black eyes.

She never thought Philip would have lied . . . never. Doubt and confusion turned slowly to the inevitable realisation that he had, and she found it difficult to draw enough breath into her lungs. 'I believed him,' she said blankly, unmindful whether she was making any sense —though she knew instinctively that Claudia would get the meaning.

'Oh, but there's nothing more irresistible to a man than having a woman who believes him!' Claudia smiled and made a little gesture as if to invite her in.

How remote she seemed, Maggie thought dully. How cool she was, how pretty in the soft fluffy pink. The sort of woman any man would want to come home to. And apparently Philip did. Without a word, she turned and walked back down the stairs she had climbed so hopefully only minutes before, back out into the cold, terrifying indifference of the city streets.

Suddenly she knew she wanted to go home to York, to her family: people she could trust and believe in, who wouldn't lie to her. Quickening her step until she was almost running, she reached the house; hurriedly she packed a few things into a bag, nearly sobbing in her frantic haste to leave and be done with this place. Depositing only the briefest of notes to Jane and Nigel on the hall table, she crept silently out of the front door. A few hours later, cramped and cold, she alighted from the bus in a heavy early morning drizzle.

There was a comfort in going home, a sense of being able to gather sufficient strength to start again. For short periods of time it was even possible to forget—then she would remember all over again, and wince at the slash of pain Philip's memory provoked. Words from love songs she had always before dismissed as foolish sentiment cut her to bits with their pathos. Sometimes she would find herself crying, without really being aware that she was.

Willingly she threw herself into the physical hard work of cleaning and polishing the old house, until her body ached with tiredness and she would fall asleep at nights from sheer exhaustion— for her father was coming home, and the wedding was to be held within days of his return. Through the days of preparation, she hid it all: the anger and the disappointment. They were easy. It was the longing that was the hardest. The longing and the knowledge that Philip would never be part of her life. Never again take her tightly into his arms, never again to feel the exultation and the perfection as their bodies came together.

Later . . . Later, when the pain was able to be borne, she would think what she should do with her life. Inevitably it would mean returning to the hospital—for a short period anyway. People said that time healed, so all she had to do then was try and live through it the best way she could.

The morning of the wedding brought with it a sadness all its own. Maggie watched the dawn skies turn overcast. A steady rain set in, and plans for a garden reception were abandoned for the largest room in the house.

'Good thing we decided on a quiet wedding,' Hadley commented cheerfully, when he came down in his old tartan dressing gown. He wasn't at all dismayed by the weather, and his obvious happiness carried Maggie through her own dark hours.

She was dressed by ten—a soft summer frock printed with pansies in many different hues of blue—and ready to receive the guests as they arrived.

She was thinking about her father when she answered the first door bell. Her face was composed in a welcoming smile. The thought that it might be Philip never entered her head.

'Hello, Maggie.' He stood on the front step, jacket collar turned up against the rain, his dark hair ruffled by the blustery north wind. The smile froze from her face. As the calm aloof eyes held hers all sense of time and reality ran away, and she had hardly began to think when her father appeared at her elbow.

'Good lord, let the man come in out of the rain, lass!' She stood dumbly aside as Philip walked in. Speechless, she watched the two men shake hands and introduce themselves. The two men who meant everything in the world to her. Nothing in her seemed to be functioning —she could not have made those introductions if her life depended on it.

'The hospital, eh?' her father was saying. 'Well, let me take your jacket. Lord, you're wet! Better come and dry off in the kitchen where it's warm.'

Why did he have to come now and ruin this day, of all days? Now, when the pain was finally beginning to dull, why did he have to come and make it raw again? If he had decided to come and offer some kind of explanation after all—well, he could forget it, because she didn't want to hear. Stunned and angry, Maggie stood by, when she should have darted forward to catch her father's arm and warn him before it was too late. Warn him that this man, with all his fine diplomacy and charm, could lie and lie and lie.

Hadley had noticed his daughter's frantic expression and had decided it was an improvement on the wooden one that had prevailed of late. Besides, he couldn't help but like the look of this man who introduced himself as her friend, and he prided himself on being a good judge of character. So he turned and said calmly to Maggie, 'Ask Brownie if there's a pot of hot coffee.'

Maggie clenched her hands at her sides. Her father knew very well they were up to their ears in last-minute preparations and that there was no time to be brewing up pots of coffee. 'Dad,' she said, through gritted teeth, 'Brownie has gone to get ready . . .' At which point Philip turned and smilingly addressed himself to her father.

'If this is an invonvenient time . . .?'

Of course it was inconvenient. How could he possibly

not see that, when they were obviously dressed for an occasion of some importance? Maggie wanted to say so, but refrained, though only out of politeness.

'Not in the least,' her father was assuring Philip heartily. 'I'm getting married later on in the morning, but there's plenty of time . . .' His eyes rested on his daughter's face, which appeared to have come so amazingly to life. 'Maggie will take you through and make a hot drink.'

Maggie managed to conceal her agitation with a shrug of indifference and a look of polite uninterest, but it was no use. Philip was wringing Hadley's hand and offering his congratulations in the best family manner, as though he were a member of it already.

'If I'm not very much mistaken,' Hadley said as a car drew up outside, 'that will be Bob Allen,' an old colleague who was acting as best man. 'He said he'd come early, we have a few things to discuss, so I'll go and let him in while you young people get reacquainted.'

There was no help for it but do as he requested. 'Come with me,' Maggie said to Philip, her eyes avoiding his. 'Would you like a cup of tea?' she asked, leading the way into the kitchen.

'Thanks, I would.' His voice was as stilted as hers. He followed her in and stood with his back to the warmth of the old Aga stove, watching as she filled the kettle and plugged it in. Her hair was brushed into a cap of curls, and her round cheeks and small sweet chin looked so vulnerable he was moved by a hot rushing protectiveness towards her.

More than ever he was riddled by anxiety, thinking she might refuse to listen, and he waited nervously. He wasn't used to either feeling, but then, everything he felt for Maggie was totally new and alien to him. Damn Claudia for making trouble! Very simply, he had allowed her the use of his bathroom when her hot water heater had failed, and while she was in his flat had slipped back to the hospital to see Beth. Claudia should have finished within an hour at the most; she was there waiting when he returned some three hours later, and her eyes let him know why. Exhausted and worried, he had been neither amused nor flattered, and had asked her to leave. If she had not come to him only the day before, in a paroxysm of guilt, he would never have known Maggie had called at his flat that evening. And now he had to explain it all. He cleared his throat cautiously.

'Maggie, I know what you must be thinking,' he said, so gently that her eyes flew up to his. Those lacy-rimmed blue-grey eyes. Oh God—his breath slowly strangled in his throat as he looked into them. Maggie's eyes.

Admit it—he was desperately in love with her. He had bought a house, fooling himself it was because he needed one now that Tim was growing up. But it was for Maggie that he had bought it, and he knew it now. He also knew that he was going to marry her. He had loved and wanted her from the time he had looked over his mask and into those clear rounded eyes on the other side of the operating table.

But marriage? He had never thought of her as old enough. He had nurtured a safe illusion of a lovely young girl, and he had not let her change his life. But as she stared at him, he was forced to see the woman she was—proud, strong, loving, a woman who was able to make her own way in life. He would be an absolute fool to think she couldn't survive without him. For all he knew, she might have already made plans.

Maggie started as the steam suddenly hissed from the kettle. 'Do you?' she said tightly, turning away. 'Or do you just imagine you know what it is I'm thinking?' As she busied herself making the tea Philip stared at her across the few feet of kitchen dividing them.

Oh God, Maggie was thinking, why did he have to come and start it all up again? She could get him out of her mind, but he had to leave her alone, long enough.

She poured the tea, and said coolly, 'It really doesn't matter to me why you thought it necessary to make this visit.' Her eyes flickered up as she passed him the cup. Those beautiful blue eyes of his that were so aware, and so hard to fool; her hands shook as he took the tea from her and she snatched them back to safety. All she wanted to do was creep away. But still she gazed into his eyes, her own revealing the love and longing for him that she could never banish from her heart. Go, Maggie told herself frantically. Go before he realises it. Go while I still can.

Philip reached her before she got to the kitchen door, spinning her round against him so hard the breath was all but knocked from her body. The sweet scent of her was in his nose and in his throat, all the weeks and weeks of longing fanned and ignited into a fire that made him feverish, as he groped blindly with his mouth for hers.

She twisted her head away, leaving a smear of lipstick, but he kept on kissing her until her arms slid up with a will of their own, locking around his neck, her mouth hungry for him, her whole body shivering and tensed. The hours and hours she had wanted him to do this, longed for him, loved him, cried.

Slowly, unwillingly they came apart, aware at last that at any moment the door might open, that guests would soon be arriving. Unbearably shy of him now, Maggie stood a little apart, her eyes lowered.

'You'd better drink your tea before it gets cold,' she said in a strange voice. And as he turned from her, she knew she would remember him this way for the rest of her life: the way his eyes crinkled at the corners when he looked at her, the shape of his long straight nose—how graceful he was! Always. For this was the end. It had to be. There was nothing he could say that would make her think otherwise. Even loving him the way she did could not make her risk her life and happiness with a man who could deceive her as he had done, and would presumably go on deceiving her.

Though these might have been her thoughts, little did she realise how her face belied them. When her father came to the door to tell her that it was time to walk across the road to the church, he saw only a beautiful young woman who was in love. He smiled and looked at Philip. 'Why don't you stay and join us? It's just going to be a quiet little ceremony. A few friends, one or two of the family, then a wedding breakfast back here . . .'

Before Maggie could make objections, the doorbell was ringing, and there was Aunty May needing to be helped up the steps and Cousin Betty shown the way to the bathroom, and the guests who didn't know each other introduced. They all welcomed Philip as one of the party, and Maggie could hardly make a scene by asking him to go.

It was a simple, beautiful little ceremony. Standing in the front pew with her posy of gardenias, Maggie watched her father slide the ring on Moira's finger and then bend his head in a tender kiss. It was too much for Maggie. A tear gathered momentum and rolled unchecked down her cheek. Why, oh, why hadn't she thought to stuff a hankie up her sleeve? Even as she was thinking it, a large silk bandanna was thrust into hand; Maggie knew very well it was Philip's handkerchief, and that he was standing close behind her. Though they were not touching, she could feel his presence.

It was over, and her father and Moira were signing the register. Because she and Philip happened to be the nearest, the Vicar asked them to sign as witnesses. Maggie stepped forward and signed her name, entering her address at the side, then handed the pen to Philip and watched absently as he wrote his name and address. And then everyone was crowding around to kiss the bride and she had to introduce Philip to Moira, who was taking a particular interest in him. Then the whole party walked back to the house, Philip in the middle of them.

But all the time there was something at the back of her mind—something that had escaped her. Suddenly she knew what it was. Above the laughter and buzz of conversation and the popping of champagne corks, she said, 'Philip . . . that isn't your address you entered in the register.'

For a moment neither of them spoke. He was standing so close to her she could feel the prickly Harris tweed of his jacket sleeve against her bare arm. Absently she thought it was still slightly damp, and that he should have waited before he put it on again.

'It's my new address,' he said huskily. His eyes met hers and time ceased to run. His voice was no more than a whisper.

'I love you, Maggie. Marry me . . .'

Maggie's mind reeled. It was what she had wanted to hear for so very long. But now? Desolately she again saw Claudia in her fluffy pink bathrobe standing in the doorway of his flat. White-lipped, her attention was jerked back to reality as Brownie clutched at her arm.

'Would your young man like to come and give me a hand with the table?' the housekeeper asked. Maggie wanted to say right back that he was not her young man. She would have, if the Vicar had not been watching.

But Philip had heard. 'Lead the way,' he said, and his smile had Brownie smiling with delight. Maggie felt the strong steady warmth of his hand on the small of her back. 'Come with me,' he said softly in her ear.

Painfully conscious of the interested looks they were getting, Maggie turned and led the way to the room that had been prepared for the wedding breakfast. Just as soon as the door closed behind them, though, she swung round. 'And then you could keep Claudia on in your flat, I suppose!' She was breathing hard, her face white and angry. 'You do believe in hedging your bets, don't you?'

There was something like desperation in Philip's eyes as he looked at her. 'Maggie darling,' he pleaded, 'please let me explain, it's all a ridiculous mistake . . .'

She wouldn't listen, she wouldn't!

'No!' she cried, and backed away, fearful that if she did, she would believe him because she wouldn't be able to help herself—as she had done the last time. Then she would be hurt, no doubt, all over again.

Philip reached out and caught her to him. 'You will listen,' he said harshly, pulling her close, his mouth against the silky tangle of curls. He could feel her fighting him, but he made her listen, telling her simply and clearly exactly what had happened.

'Oh,' she said, mumbling into his shirt when he had finished. 'And of course, when you came back and found her still there, you sent her straight back up to her flat, I suppose.' She had meant to be sarcastic, but her voice sounded rather more hopeful than anything.

Philip wrapped his arms around her tightly and said, 'Darned right I did! And if you think she was waiting for me in a diaphanous négligé, you'd be right again. She was.' Then his voice changed, became urgent, and he held her apart and looked down at her with eyes brilliant with love.

'Maggie, you're running away from your own fear of being hurt. You have to stop and turn around and see that I love you and—God help me,' his voice broke in a note of despair, 'need you, Maggie.'

'Oh, Philip!' All the love she felt for him flowed into those two words, and she was crying and laughing at once, choking on her sobs. 'Oh, Philip . . .' was all she could say. Then the door opened and Brownie came bustling in.

'I thought we could shift the table over so the French windows could be opened, then people can go out and in as they please,' she said, seemingly oblivious to their startled looks.

It was then that Maggie noticed the rain had stopped. A watery sun was beginning to struggle through, and the air was warm again, and full of the noise of birds and insects. When the table and chairs were as Brownie wanted and she had departed once more, Maggie went over and opened the windows, letting in a tide of musky scent from the wet Italian laurels. Philip joined her, and they stood side by side.

Those few moments were precious; it was enough just to stand beside him, share his thoughts, be part of his solitude. For Maggie no longer felt shut away from him—and most important of all, she believed him.

Philip put his arm around her waist, as he told her that Claudia was planning to resign and go back to the States. He said in a husky undertone, 'It would be the best thing that could happen for all of us. She was jealous and obstructive from the start—I must have been blind not to have seen it.' Looking down at her, his eyes became tender. 'If you want the job, Maggie, it's yours.'

'Now which job is that, sir?' she asked with a quick teasing smile. 'Your wife, or your Theatre Sister?'

A wide spontaneous smile broke out, erasing disciplined years from his features. 'Both,' he said, and laughed softly. 'But don't think you get any choice with the former. The latter you can think about, but not for too long—we need you back.' His eyes glowed with love for her, and pride. For all Maggie's inexperience, she had proved she could run an operating theatre. She had welded that place into a happy working unit, something Claudia had never been able to do.

'You think we can work together professionally, as man and wife?' Maggie asked, smiling through tears of sheer happiness because she had no doubts, she just wanted to hear Philip tell her so himself.

'We'll cope,' he said laconically, and when her eyes went anxiously to his face, he grinned and hugged her. 'There'll be problems, it wouldn't be a marriage or an operating theatre without them, but I don't doubt our ability to solve them. There,' he said with amusement, 'satisfied?' For a moment they stood in happy silence.

'There won't be many of us left,' Maggie said quite suddenly. 'Jane going to Canada, Duncan off to New Zealand and Gary planning on working in the States.'

'Don't count on Gary leaving just yet,' he told her with a laugh, relieved to hear her talk as though she were part of the team again. 'I've spoken with him, and he's applying for his old job again. I'll make that young hound into a surgeon yet! I saw him yesterday, by the way, and he sends his regards to you, and he also mentioned something about the blue pullover he happened to be wearing—said you'd understand . . .' He looked down at her and was astonished to see both tears and laughter.

But there was a question Maggie had not yet asked, one she wanted to badly, and as the expressions flew across her face, he knew what it was. 'Beth is fine,' he told her, and took her hand in his, holding on to it tightly. 'She and Harry got married, he spends all the time he can with her and they seem remarkably happy. There's something else too that you should know. Beth is pregnant.'

'Pregnant?' Maggie's grey eyes flashed to his. He nodded, smiling. 'She's thrilled to bits about it, so is Harry. If they have a daughter, she'll be named Maggie after you, and a son . . . Well, you'll never guess who he's going to be called after!'

Maggie could and her eyes told him so. 'That's wonderful news! A baby will make all the difference, give her everything to live for. Oh, please God, let her get well and strong.' Philip's face was filled with the gentleness that was so much part of his strength and that made Maggie ache with love and tenderness, she reached up for him and felt the utter pleasure of being gathered tight in his arms.

'If it has anything to do with us, she will be,' he said, his voice husky with an emotion he was more used to keeping bottled up inside. Maggie buried her face deep in his chest and he stroked her hair. 'Beth wants you there when she has her last operation—she told me so.'

All this time Maggie had not realised how worried she had been about Beth. To have it spirited away with this good news was such a relief. She took a long breath of rain-scented air and felt it go right to the bottom of her lungs. There was something else, equally important, if not more so. 'And Tim?' she asked, searching his eyes.

Philip had made her so happy, happier than she had ever been. But it had to be right for Tim, or he would regret it, and she couldn't bear it if he did that, she loved him so much. 'What will Tim think if we get married?' she asked.

'When we get married,' Philip corrected her, hugging her close. 'More likely it's what he'll say if we don't,' he told her with a wide grin. 'The way he talks, he can't wait to show you off to his friends!'

Cradled in the loving intimacy of his arms, Maggie's happiness was complete. As they kissed and murmured endearments, sounds of laughter came to them from the lawn at the front of the house. Maggie could hear Rufus barking excitedly and she said, 'I think the photographs are being taken, we'd better go and join them . . .'

Philip held her at arm's length and gazed with fierce longing at her precious face. 'I'm not letting you go until I get an answer,' he declared in a husky voice. 'And you can say anything you want, so long as it's yes!'

Maggie looked up into his eyes and saw the same love burning in the deep blue as was in her own. For a moment she couldn't say or do a thing, except slide her arms up and around his neck. 'Oh yes, yes, my darling,' she whispered, her throat choked with emotion, 'I'll marry you and be your wife.'

'Maggie!' He caught her tightly to him, never again to be kept from holding her so.

The Perfect Gift.

Four new exciting novels from Mills and Boon:
SOME SORT OF SPELL – by Frances Roding
– An enchantment that couldn't last or could it?
MISTRESS OF PILLATORO – by Emma Darcy
– The spectacular setting for an unexpected romance.
STRICTLY BUSINESS – by Leigh Michaels
– highlights the shifting relationship between friends.
A GENTLE AWAKENING – by Betty Neels
– demonstrates the truth of the old adage 'the way to a man's heart…'

Make Mother's Day special with this perfect gift.
Available February 1988. Price: £4.80

Mills & Boon

From: Boots, Martins, John Menzies, W H Smith, Woolworths and other paperback stockists.